I0641207

The Herders' Chapel

A novel by

Matti Aikio

Translated by John Weinstock
Introduction by Gunnar Gjengset

Agarita Press

Set in Minion Pro

The original of this book was published as

Hyrdernes Kapel

Roman

Forlagt av H. Aschehoug & Co.
Kristiania 1918

Cover design by John Weinstock and Beth Brotherton

Ollu giitu dáid olbmuide hui buori veahki ovddas:
Reidar Rødland, Harald Gaski, Gunnar Gjengset

This translation has been published with
the financial support of NORLA.

The Herders' Chapel

Matti Aikio's The Herders' Chapel

An introduction by Gunnar Gjengset, Phil. Dr.

My interest in Matti Aikio's authorship has an overarching goal: to mediate his zeal to create an idea about the Sámi as a distinctive people with its own language, its own culture and history. Aikio's project was to constitute the Sámi people as subject of their own narrative. In Aikio's authorship, which extended from 1904 to 1929, this was a highly risky project. Aikio's public was largely Norwegian as well as Sámi who were literate and knew Norwegian. The Norwegian readers would gladly have had their prejudices about Norwegian heroes and easily duped Sámi confirmed, but themselves were easily duped by the Sámi Aikio who let various Sámi characters make fun of Norwegians throughout his entire authorship. During an age especially hostile to aboriginal people Aikio's explorations of borders for the development of ethnicity and culture were rather daring – and Aikio carefully investigates these borders throughout his entire authorship, at the same time as the borders are expanding.

With his fifth novel Aikio anticipated the distinctively Norwegian Easter crime fiction tradition with what else but an Easter crime in *The Herders' Chapel* (1918). As usual Aikio operates with a clever title: where is *The Herders' Chapel*? And not least: Who are 'the herders'? And the information that the chapel lies in *Helligskogen* sharpens the curiosity about who the herders might be. Which accordingly cannot prevent a contagion from spreading that leads to an outbreak of illness for sixteen people and eleven deaths, plus one – in spite of the sacrosanct name of the place. But here I am anticipating the summary and analysis, which I have suggested would focus on how cultures in contact absolutely can transmit harmful contagion. This situation will be compared with the development of Matti Aikio's ethnic consciousness, after the reception of the book is discussed. But first a brief look at the short story that underlies *The Herders' Chapel*.

The short story "The chapel in the wilderness," is actually the model for this novel – printed in *Tidens Tegn* in 1916.[1] The chapel functions at the same time as a mountain hostel for reindeer herders on the move who usually spend the Easter festivities here. The purpose of the short story seems to be to point out that large portions of the Sámi area were legally still a sort of no-man's-land. In the Sámi myth at the basis, the hero is a mountain Sámi who lives at Sørøya in Skibotn in North Troms. With the reindeer Bižus and a birch bark torch he tricks Karelians on a plunder expedition off a cliff:

> When the path became so steep that it was no longer possible for people to walk down, the mountain Sámi suddenly threw himself to the side […] and let Bižus with the rein and birch bark torch go down through the cleft, and the Karelians followed along as the mountain Sámi said they should do, and thus they all fell to their deaths (Brita Pollan, 1999).

This central Sámi legend is mentioned only in a subordinate clause in Aikio's short story from 1916, but the way he uses the story attests to his wishing to draw attention to the common mythical features in the legend: it is actually a universal story about how an inferior minority protects itself against powerful intruders. The core of the short story is this: how the mountain hostel/chapel host, the returned Sámi Olle Gauvoine, did not entirely manage to reorient himself compared to the Sámi people's time-honored behavior: "Thus ended Olle Gauvoine's apostle work. He headed south again and became a pastor in the free temple."

A half year after this short story was in print, the negotiations began between the Zionist Chaim Weizmann and the British government on the formation of a colony for the Jews in Palestine, and the day before that the Sámi national meeting in Trondheim opened. This coincidence was entirely fortuitous, but in posterity it can appear as a single idea. As far as Matti Aikio was concerned the history from Hamburg in 1909 looked like it was recurring (he was staying in Hamburg at the same time as a Zionist congress was held there): he finds himself in places in the world where important historical events are going to take place, but chooses to trivialize his presence. Either by ridiculing it as when he wrote that he took a job as a reindeer driver in Hagenbeck's zoo in Hamburg in 1909, or by claiming he was in Trondheim to write about the Nidaros cathedral in 1917.

But Aikio's long-range strategy had a goal that *resembled* the Zionists': an independent area for one's own people, but not total independence. By 'independent' it appears Aikio meant the right to speak their own language and maintain their own culture, accordingly be construed by the outside world as Sámi, just as the Jews in a new Palestine would be construed as Zionists – Jews settled in the historic Zion.

Tuesday February 6, 1917 Norway was asked to ally itself with the USA by President Woodrow Wilson. The same day Aikio was present at the Phoenix hotel in Trondheim to attend the first large Sámi national meeting constituted that same

---

[1] *Tidens Tegn*, Kristiania 6/13/1916.

afternoon. Aikio made only one report from the Sámi national meeting. It was nevertheless maybe not so strange when one thinks of the delicate double bind he found himself in: if he expressed support for the Sámi demands he could risk losing his Norwegian public. And if he defended the rulers' policies, the Sámi could declare that Matti Aikio in no way represented their points of view. In such a situation it would be smartest to hold his tongue. Therefore, he wrote just the one article.

In Matti Aikio's catalog therefore we will find a chapel that surrounds this first Sámi national meeting: the short story "The chapel in the wilderness" was written in 1916, and was rewritten in novel format with *The Herders' Chapel* in 1918. Both texts depicted emigrant Sámi's abortive homecomings to their original Sámi environments, and both discussed the consequences of the hegemon's encroaching culture. After the national meeting in 1917 it was natural for Aikio to warn that an incorrect strategy vis-à-vis the larger society could have serious consequences.

In 1918 the book came out, after several rounds with the publisher since Aikio had sent in the manuscript the year before. Here follows a summary of the action: Matti Aikio with this text was back close to his childhood tracts. True enough he placed the text's Herders' Chapel near Helligskogen, a place in North Troms and thereby on the outskirts of the Finnmark plateaus, but a place that functioned as a neutral meeting place for the two competing Sámi groups from Karasjok and Kautokeino: "The inscriptions on a large border stone some miles south of Helligskogen tell that here the three kingdoms meet."[2]

The text's geographical placement is thereby apparently not problematic: there is a mountain hostel in Skibotn valley by the name of Helligskogen. It is a common wooden structure, but today is not set up as a chapel. The place lies ten to fifteen miles from the three national borders that are mentioned in the text. It is also a short ways to the sea, so that one "used to pole the ninety miles up here to Helligskogen" (19). The place had for a long time been a center for the reindeer Sámi's migrations in these tracts during the winter.

Helligskogen in Skibotn valley lies in Storfjord municipality, and "the mountain hostel lies along E8 toward Finland, about 30 km from Skibotn and 10 km from the national border" (from a local brochure), and has been one of the national mountain hostels since 1848. Whether or not it is correct to say the place once had been a 'Sámi sacrificial site,' the name 'Helligskogen' is explained that way.

The action in the book is quite complex for a novel of limited format, something many critics also pointed out. The main character is the Sámi Jansa Olle who becomes a dentist in Kristiania and calls himself Ole Janssen. When the action in the book begins, he takes on the job as hostel host at the aforementioned mountain hostel in Helligskogen, and the reason is "conversion? – religious crisis? – schizoid personality disorder? – failure at life? – sentimental homesickness? No, No, there

[2] Aikio 1918:12. Quotations will be given consecutively in the text with page references.

one will not find Ole Janssen" (16). The author is not of much help here, but suggests that Janssen is lacking nothing, for he had "never overcome the virile basic trait in the so-called view of life" (ibid.). On the contrary he suffered from periodic "fear of life – the one that had pursued him throughout his life and already in his childhood years allowed him to experience the fears of the tremor" (ibid.).

Earlier he practiced a couple years in a small eastern coastal town at the same time as he worked on an aesthetic-philosophical treatise. He tires of his bourgeois life in the small town, moves to Kristiania and experiences that his treatise gives him a kick-start; he "barged straight into the capital's Bohemian life" (16) Thereby the fear of life also vanished. He led a life of riot and revel for a couple years.

> And then somehow the enchantment was suddenly gone. The fear of life said hello and thanks for our last time together [...] And now the old shadow returned from the dead in the conglomeration of Asian and sorcery that was his countenance, his entire character and being. (ibid.)

Ole Janssen, alias Jansa Olle, struggles with existential torments that quite concretely reach bottom in his ethnic obsessions. He struggles with a new treatise, tries to write a little for the newspapers, "but gets nowhere" (ibid.). Then he opens a practice in the capital, "And it doesn't go any better with his dental skill [...] ends up in the little eastern coastal town" (ibid.). But now happily married, to Agnete. He tries to finish the work *Cheerful Tenacity*, but the fear returns. He comes up with ideas that his wife is unfaithful, at the same time as he feels something is wrong with his right arm, because he has "every so often felt some bad warnings in it" (17). A professional psychologist would surely have suggested something about psychosomatic illness here; he cultivates an imagined jealousy at the same time as his right arm gets lame. He uses the same strategy on Agnete as Captain Steen used against his wife in King Ahab – silence: "Morning after morning she appeared at the breakfast table with a red-eyed and swollen face." (18)

Mrs. Steen died from it, but Agnete chooses another strategy. When Ole Janssen asks her to go see a doctor for her illness she takes him at his word: "But one day she showed up with the doctor" (18), a contrary action that Janssen oddly enough considers a victory: "and it became his Pyrrhic victory" (ibid.), for "He is threatened by a breakdown" (ibid.). But Agnete proclaims: "I'm leaving tomorrow" (ibid.), and is therefore more in line with Ibsen's Nora. She leaves him; he nearly loses his wits, and loses the use of his arm: "but his hand, the right hand, doesn't want to ... it had become paralyzed." (19) After that "he was driven away – into the long night." (ibid.), for a lengthy stay in institution.

Before things got so far, he had been busy with dental work, received a couple letters from Agnete, and written on the treatise. It is a "eulogy to cynicism, materialism, bourgeoisie [...] a gateway into his deeply harmonic philosophy of life [...] if one wants the end, one must also want the means" (ibid.) And if the goal in life is the flower, the means must be "the fat, strong smelling manure" (ibid.). With the title

Cheerful Tenacity one inevitably makes associations to Friedrich Nietzsche and his work The Gay Science from 1882;[3] it is of course an author and a philosopher that would better fit into 'the capital's Bohemian life' in the period around 1915.

After a couple years convalescence the main character is in the middle of the book's present time layer. Ole Janssen has misused friends and contacts to get the position as house host at the mountain hostel in Helligskogen, and the driver Bittoš Hansa is transporting Jansa Olle up to the new structure. Back in Sámiland Aikio's everlasting conflict between what he calls 'the east parish' and 'the west (plateau) parish' slips into place.[4] Yet he avoids his home village: "why didn't you travel through your home village?" (32) Jauna Jauna asks, who is also from there. Olle clearly has something unfinished with his home village. At the same time, he is torn between city and country, that is, between ethnicities: his former Norwegian wife writes without fail and wants/doesn't want him back.

Ole Janssen/Jansa Olle also struggles with professionalism: as a 'Norwegian' educated college graduate, it is expected in the Sámi environment that he can exceed his credentials. Since he "too was allowed to mount the pulpit" (31), it is expected that he give sermons from there, a church function reserved for fully ordained pastors. He does it then also on request, but that sort of hubris is severely punished: the clergy relieved him from the job. But it happens only after he has tried to introduce an urbane hygiene regimen in the mountains – an attempt that has fatal consequences. A contributory factor is also that he had a live-in relationship with Aile, before he was legally separated from his wife. He committed a crime against various laws, and thereby was politely asked to leave his position.

Ole Janssen's transformation back to Sámi culture creates conflicts. Several Sámi he associates with have one and all quit drinking and reindeer theft. Almost to test them Janssen sets a bottle of brandy on the table. The driver Bittoš Hansa and reindeer owner Jauna Jauna assert their abstinence, but since Bittoš Hansa thinks Olle doubts his sincerity, he finally steals the bottle: "Had you been a true gentleman you would have offered me a nip […] You are the most wretched coward I have met in my life." (36) Olle sets after him; they fight and the booze runs out into the snow. Bittoš Hansa eats up the slush, and dies from the acute cold shock: "That whole quantity of snow slush the brandy had tempted him to slurp into himself had been too much for his stomach and intestines." (44) One can assert that because someone found the body, like a "a rolled up heap of reindeer jacket lying on the sled road. It was Bittoš Hansa. He was dead" (ibid.).

---

[3] Although the philosophy sketched here would better fit Kant's moral philosophy than the nihilism Nietzsche investigates: http://www.nietzschesource.org/texts/eKGWB/FW.

[4] During Matti Aikio's time there was antagonism between Aikio's home village Karasjok and Kautokeino. In Aikio's literary universe Kautokeino is often mentioned as 'the west plateau parish,' and the inhabitants from here are called somewhat condescending 'the magpie people' (see below).

It seems as if Jansa Olle tries to trivialize this death: "What did it concern him that a Bittoš Hansa drank himself to death on brandy slush –" (77). But it turns out this death haunts others than Olle. The herder Nilas who "had left with Bittoš Hansa's body" (78) said he had been exposed to a mishap with the coffin when they crossed the ice on Deadman's Lake: "Then it was as if a heavy crash went through the ice on the lake" (80), and the morning after Nilas discovered "that both the body and the sled were gone" (ibid.). When summer neared it was decided not to look further for Bittoš Hansa's body, but Nilas went back with Olle from Jauna Jauna's si-ida: "They looked everywhere around Deadman's Lake, unfortunately in vain." (83)

But this doesn't change Olle's well-being in his new existence, "he doesn't feel any of the insidious anxiety" (39) which has long plagued him. It is remnants of epilepsy that afflicted him as a child, but "The attacks had stopped in his fourteenth year" (36). On the contrary, he was cast as a possible husband for Jauna Jauna's daughter Aile who really ought to have a better match in the East Parish Erki Lemik Issak's son – or even with Saivo Piera, son of the West Parish's old Saivo, because "the Saivo family was the pure exception among the West Parish folks" (44). Aile's sister Gudnel is married to "Little-Andi as he was also called by the family" (43). She teases her unmarried sister and speaks warmly about Saivo Piera, "the son in this marvelous family" (44), and suggests she ought to travel down to the village at Easter to meet him. Something Aile refuses.

But it is difficult for Olle to see himself as Aile's suitor because of his far greater age and the boring fact that he is already married, and at the same time is tormented by Bittoš Hansa's death. In other words: Ole Janssen/Jansa Olle finds himself in the middle of an existential crisis, now also as having returned to Sámiland:

> No, my fate is not my fate. It is only my evil, dismal shadow that can hit on playing tricks with yellow slush – not to punish Bittoš Hansa – the one who dies doesn't suffer evil from dying – but to fan myself on the nose with the reflection from the confounded world.

> I no longer acknowledge my fate and will not allow myself to be browbeaten by its pranks. I've become a grown man now. (49)

However, neither Janssen nor his creator Aikio wants to let the reader in on the meaning of the assertion "my fate is not my fate" (ibid.). But the assertion is sur-rounded by Janssen reading chapters of his unpublished treatise: "And Olle reads one more chapter in 'Cheerful Tenacity.' (ibid.). Janssen suggests here that the inci-dent with the brandy and Bittoš Hansa was an episode in a past stage of his life. Then he let fate prevail. Now he had on the contrary left this life, written a philosophical treatise we may presume deals with hardening oneself by taking fate into one's own hands. And now he is well situated in another phase of his life: back in the realm of his childhood, or in any case right next to it, as a grown up and mature man, in other words. Ole Janssen takes command over fate, and he will not let himself be 'browbeaten by its unforeseen obstacles.' He can choose the adequate behavior; he is a grown man now. But the text wants to demonstrate that there is distance between choice of one own behavior and attempts to transplant the same behavior to a foreign milieu.

In this introduction I have tried to show how Aikio with The Herders' Chapel delivered a book about an indigenous person[5] who is an outsider, outside both in the capital and small towns in the central districts, and as one returning home in his original milieu. In an attempt to realize a culture's third space, in accordance with postcolonial methods, in the text's 'Helligskogen,' he has the misfortune of causing a number of people's deaths. As an educated dentist he manages to create himself a career in the hegemon's society with the help of successful mimicry. When he tries to return to Sámiland to launch adaptations from urbanity that can improve the subalterns' every day, his actions result in pure mockery. Also because he places himself beyond the universal moral codex by living with a concubine.

The book discusses how unreflective Sámi can function as mortally dangerous agents for urbanity, and thereby this is a book about contagion. In an elegant way, that unfortunately escaped the contemporary Norwegian critics, he gave a mission to his Sámi critics. The year before they had publically branded Aikio as a traitor, because of his pronouncements to the press on the occasion of history's first Norwegian Sámi national meeting in Trondheim in 1917 (see above). With the description of Jansa Olle/Ole Janssen's behavior in Sámiland, Aikio is saying: now listen – we mean the same thing: the hegemon represents a permanent danger for the Sámi minority. But my analysis is more correct, Aikio asserts in accordance with my interpretation: we must seek consensus rather than confrontation in today's situation, just by insisting on our own cultural practice can we avoid the greater society's detrimental contagion. Overly unrealistic demands can lead to segregation or heavy-handed assimilation.

In spite of its modest dimensions, The Herders' Chapel marks a significant development in the somewhat static conception of ethnic contrasts we find in Aikio's four previous books, where "Race sets Borders." Now Aikio warns that a cultural transformation is setting in, in spite of pronounced resistance against Norwegianization. The plastered Norwegians on the platform can just as well be merged with Sámi, as light-haired and blue-eyed Sámi can have gotten Norwegian blood. The book's message is thereby that the most important thing for the Sámi people vis-à-vis the threat from the larger society is to take care of Sámi culture. Language and attire is more important than ethnicity. Then Aikio doesn't see it in such a way that it is only the city and modernity pouring into Sámiland – in good postcolonial understanding

---

[5]"Indigenous; originating in and characteristic of a particular region or country; native, *the indigenous peoples of southern Africa*," http://dictionary.reference.com/browse/indigenous.

Sámiland is also trickling into the hegemon's culture. The text's third room thereby becomes the open road communication and cultural contact must have between the hegemon and the subaltern minority.

Thereby this book ends with an increasing optimism, and is therefore more dynamic than the preceding books. And this is a sensational conclusion in the middle of a world war: over time cultures will mix in peaceful and natural ways, and ethnic contrasts will be lessened. The development moves on, and "The train whistles …" (138).

On the perilous crossing of the mountains

Two men are driving with reindeer sled over a bumpy mountain plateau beneath the polar sky – late in March. They're driving eastward; behind them glows a large evening sun in a cold and bright sky; its reflection sparkles in long, reddish streaks over the ridges on the range of hills, and it blazes so simply and strongly against the blue shadows from the hollows where the tops of the dwarf birch and willow barely reach above the snowdrifts – there are in any case a few dark bush spots here and there which the eye can rest on in the middle of all this sun and snow and blazing blue sky.

Some ptarmigans stand at cheerful attention right by the curved groove of a sled road and curiously watch the travelers – there are still creatures in God's unsoiled nature for whom fear of humans has not been inherited.

… The one in front is the driver and his name is Bittoš Hansa. He has a few reindeer behind him; they are each pulling a sled with the traveler's personal property – except for the last one which is a braking reindeer: every time it begins to go down a steeper incline, the reindeer invariably tightens the rein so the sled in front it is tied to can't pick up speed and run between the legs of the reindeer in front – and that's how order is maintained in the whole line. Otherwise, any speed down a hill with such a string[1] would be connected to all sorts of calamities and world disturbances. Instead of shafts, one just uses, you see, a single pulling strap between the back legs of the reindeeer; this strap is fastened to a curved crossbar under the belly, a sort of belly band.

The traveler rides behind the string. His name is Ole Janssen – has been called that half a score of years – during his childhood and youth he was generally called Jansa Olle.

He has pulled himself deep down into the large reindeer jacket where he leans back in the sled – he knows how to get comfortable for sure. The breeze toys with a cockscomb of red decorated ribbon in his brand new otter skin cap with the large, four-sided crown filled with eider down. He lies and yoiks, with tobacco pipe in his mouth. The small yoik sounds he thought he had forgotten long ago, all appear to him.

---

[1] String – a line of reindeer each with its own load. A single person can have a string of up to eight-ten reindeer.

Up to now Ole Janssen has been a dentist; but at this moment he is no longer that. He is going to take over a new position; he has gotten a regular public appointment as host at a mountain hostel in Helligskogen – with obligation every Sunday and when otherwise convenient to lead devotions in the chapel the state recently has built for the reindeer Sámi who during the winter stay in these desolate but moss-covered districts and for whom it is difficult to reach their respective and as much as one hundred ten mile distant inland villages up there under the polar sky. The inscriptions on a large border stone some miles south of Helligskogen read that here the three kingdoms meet.

… Conversion? – religious crisis? – schizoid personality disorder? – failure at life? – sentimental homesickness?

No, there one will not find Ole Janssen. Unsettled and almost constantly in the force of chance he had, all the same, never overcome the virile basic trait in the so-called view of life.

Dentist Ole Janssen had practiced a couple years in a small eastern coastal town when he suddenly and unexpectedly served up an aesthetic-philosophical treatise; it created a stir and a genuine admiration; he won outright: he barged straight into the capital's Bohemian life – a happy barbarian who seemed to feel just as naturally and pleasantly well everywhere … during the small, quiet pauses he hardly had time to think about his fortunately vanished fear of life – the one that had pursued him throughout his life and already in his childhood years allowed him to experience the fears of the tremor.

For a couple of years Ole Janssen went on celebrating at life's table and in its feather quilts.

And then somehow the enchantment was suddenly gone. The fear of life said hello and thanks for our last time together. Oh no, my friend – it won't be all that easy; we'll surely simply have to join forces again!

And now the old shadow returned from the dead in the conglomeration of Asian and sorcery that was his countenance, his entire character and being. Now he again managed to tidy up thoroughly around himself, on purpose or against his will, surely mostly against his will. A few could stop him for a moment on the street and ask how it was going. Fine thanks, not so bad.

He tries to write one or other newspaper article, but gets nowhere, and the tiny bit he slaps together is not worth anything at all. And if he occasionally runs into the old parties … no, one can be silent about that; our Lord does that too – he in whose house we act badly.

He who during the two years of enchantment had something of a man of the world's unconscious self-confidence about himself, has now become helplessly tactless, clumsy, shy – he recognizes it himself; he is himself witness to the misery, but can do nothing about it.

And it doesn't go any better with his dental skill; it happens a filling comes out of a tooth even before the patient has gone out the door, well, it happens that patients who 'think for themselves' jump up from the rack and ask how in hottest hell he could have hit on becoming a dentist – seeing that a manure pitch fork seems to have been destined to be his right and only instrument.

He himself was the last one to want to concede he was a victim of spiritual poisoning – and who in his position would make that kind of admission? – no, it was just a matter of once again finding the right point of departure, the constructive element in one … oh, good grief, he finally found himself crouched in a corner like a frightened mouse half on the way to giving up … maybe it was this corner that was the point of departure? Of course, damn it! – and then it was a matter of throwing himself into the wild dance again.

… But Ole Janssen once again ends up in the little eastern coastal town. Now he is married, and he is even what one calls happily married. He has in mind to complete a large scale written work 'Cheerful Tenacity.' It is no casual idea that has occurred to him; he is and remains a strict, but freely creative systematizer, a positive moralist up to the passionate.

If only his right arm hadn't become paralyzed before … he has every so often felt some bad warnings in it.

… One evening he is sitting in his workroom, so happily tired after the day's intense work he actually enjoys this nervous consciousness afterwards that continues to work on its own after he himself is on free time. Agnete is out on a little evening stroll with her childhood friend, a doctor in town.

And while he is sitting there, a thought occurs to him that startles him … not because he believes he has gotten it for some reason, but from an involuntary fear it will obsess him. He gets up and seriously sets to work on himself … that sort of notion one has to watch out for; they have to be caught red-handed and disarmed in time.

But when Agnete gets back again around twelve, he is nevertheless unable to refrain from tasting the bitter fruit, works himself up to brush her with a couple veiled, suspicious words; he looks critically at her and remains silent … She sees it, hears it, perceives it and thinks it is ticklingly funny; she lets a touch of something concealed and guilty drift over her white face – by the living God, she is even capable of becoming confused, honestly confused.

The day after she pretended to be ignorant of the situation – as if the whole thing was just a joke that no longer was funny, and she promised herself she wouldn't let herself in for that sort of thing.

But he continued to mope. Well, let him do that, she thought; he will soon get bored with it. But then when she discovered he, in dead earnest, had become possessed, poisoned, she took him to task and was perhaps also a little affected in her sulkiness.

… Oh no, he was aware of that sort of trick.

Maybe – certainly, let us say, it could happen these two people, if there really had been something serious threatening their happiness, would have been able to save themselves in time – reality has such a great ability to remind one of the instinct of self-preservation.

But now he somehow could afford to cultivate his feelings of being poisoned, and before he knew it, he had become a helpless victim of this strong feeling – he fanned the flames at every possible and impossible opportunity – like an alcoholic who doesn't shrink from any occasion to get hold of the redeeming poison.

He had begun to sleep inside his workroom; he had to work at night, he said, and she had to sleep undisturbed. He was polite and considerate like the devil himself. Morning after morning she appeared at the breakfast table with red-eyed and swollen face. And he asked her so sincerely and objectively to try to use sleeping pills and consult the doctor.

Two evenings in succession she found a pretext to go in to him; she was in night-clothes, more lovely than ever, she knows inwardly; she is standing on the floor, he is lying down reading. Yes, it was probably best she bought those eggs, he answers – and keeps a sharp lookout his glance doesn't graze her.

And she didn't come in to him again in that garb which otherwise had been for him what David's harp was for Saul.

But one day she showed up with the doctor, while he sat in the living room. She was effervescently cheerful, and the doctor was just as brazen – so very brazen as an educated man can allow himself to be without being vulgar. But Janssen disarmed them both with the most elegant coldbloodedness.

Now he had seriously foisted a defeat on her in earnest, and it became his Pyrrhic victory; he understood it himself too immediately afterwards when he was alone. Reality began to be dangerous for him, and he had used his power of resistance in advance.

He is threatened by a breakdown – and maybe, yes maybe, a fait accompli in this direction and at this point in time would have been able to avert the fateful. But already the same evening she comes in to him, this time fully clothed.

"I'm leaving tomorrow."

"And where to?" he asks, and he is to his surprise entirely master of himself.

"I'm leaving without a route."

He sits and scratches himself on the chin with the tip of the penholder.

"But you must have money for travel. You'll get that money, I can spare it."

"Thanks, but I have money myself."

"Well, then it's another matter … As a matter of fact I hadn't known that."

"No, but that's probably not the only thing you don't know. Good night."

"Good night."

— —

And now something remarkable happens: there isn't the slightest sign he is going to collapse … Well there goes the doctor – so he hasn't run off with her.

No, he doesn't collapse; he just has the feeling he is living in a world glimmering red, and he is hectically in the mood for work. He takes care of good people's teeth and writes on 'Cheerful Tenacity,' a systematic treatise which with a tickling shudder he is witness to that turns out to be a hectic eulogy of cynicism, materialism, bourgeoisie and all the other terrifying concepts of like sort. It is not an assumed device of his; it is a gateway into his deeply harmonic philosophy of life – mankind must go over this Via Dolorosa; if one wants the end, one must also want the means. And as true as the goal in life is the flower – what in the hell should it be otherwise? – the means is and must be the fat, strong smelling manure. Let the flesh chew the cud in peace, and no untimely disturbances of the digestion! he must request. It's just zealous imitators and white-clad old women who can hit on fastening paper roses on last year's tufts of hair. Here, of course, there isn't a hint of the smell of fermenting decay yet – nothing but blushing vitality and active appetite, wherever the eye might turn!

In the middle of the summer heat he sits the whole day inside his workroom that faces south and feels no need to go out. Every evening he drinks his two glasses of green absinthe and water, never more than that. Well, he can catch himself harboring a certain suspicion of himself … he who before hadn't wanted anything to do with anything regular of that kind, he is now self-control itself. But this is of course also a life and death struggle, he says. And he can surprise himself while bending over a patient with the forceps pressed into a grip on a molar by standing there to observe 'cheerful tenacity' in the patient's face before he squeezes.

He has gotten a couple letters from Agnete, two proper, polite business letters, and he has answered them politely and properly.

Then one more came – with an unfeigned plea that he still had to try to come to his senses. He didn't reply, didn't want to reply to it – one has to be careful of one's finger.

He still drinks just the two glasses of green absinthe and water in the evening and works with a greater strength than ever before. His attitude and countenance have become a lion's; he is tempted to be dismayed at all this resistance.

It has already turned autumn. One morning he opens his eyes in fear, in bewilderment … really, thank goodness, it was just a dream: – someone knocking on the window … of course, it must have just been a dream … he gets up and opens the window, and down there in the dark he glimpses Agnete's face. You're wrong, he says, you don't live here. And he closes the window.

Of course, it must have been a dream … he lies bathed in sweat. Then he suddenly becomes wide awake; he jumps up – merciful God, it has been dreadful reality! He wants to grab his clothes that are draped on the chair, but his hand, the right hand, doesn't want to … it had become paralyzed.

A few hours later he was driven away – into the long night.

What God wants, he wants too; his will is a difficult will.

On the marriages of Lapps by means of fire

And now the former dentist Ole Janssen is driving over a bumpy mountain plateau beneath the polar sky, while the sun is starting to sink down into the earth.

He has been a convalescent for a couple years. His right arm is still paralyzed, but no worse than that it sometimes can help the left one. And he has absolute control over his 'mind'; the crisis had, in any case in its present form, almost been just acute.

It's been three weeks since he left his last residence down south. Fourteen days ago he had traveled up from a marketplace down by the sea, at the bottom of one of the long fjords up here. He had stopped a couple days in one of them, at the western of the two inland villages here in the closed, large emptiness. The two last nights he had slept in the tents of some mountain Sámi he had met en route, in some small valley hollows here on this plateau.

… It begins to slope downward. A long, blue dusk climbs up from the valley in front of them. Birch and willow scrubs become denser and taller.

They reach a steep slope, and here the valley opens up. And here the driver stops, Bittoš Hansa, and shouts to Jansa Olle as the gentleman has begun to be called:

"There you see your church, Olle, and your house."

Yes, it was a real church they saw down there in the valley floor, a little chapel with steeple and spire and cross. A bit away from it was 'the farmhouse,' a storehouse and a barn structure.

This, Olle's future home, lay up on a riverbank with a rather level plain behind.

There were large pine hillsides on both sides of the river which now was just a long and curvy stripe of snow down into the valley bottom. There were two valleys that collided here, just a mile and a half above the cluster of houses.

The plain down there Olle had heard about as a child – from the salmon fishermen down in the village who a few summers used to pole the ninety miles up here to Helligskogen: but then it was also boys who could pole and boats that could be poled – they could go like arrows up over the worst rapids.

Such a plain is a good defense; it gives space for the mind and keeps everything stealthy at a distance … as well as a plain can do that.

It is this place that is called Helligskogen,[2] an old sacrificial place now adorned by a little chapel with cross and spire. Inside a circle with radius of a hundred miles there isn't a single resident otherwise; there are just some winter tents of thick weave sending a little smoke up from some valley hollows on the plateau or from a wooded hillside in the main valley.

But Olle took comfort in the river being the same as flowed past the village down there …

When the houses and chapel were built last year it was the intention of getting a Sámi farming family from down in the village to settle here in Helligskogen; here over time as many cows could be fed as desired; here were salmon and trout and whitefish in the rivers and in the mountain lakes – not to mention meat that for a song could be bartered from the mountain Sámi. And besides three hundred crowns in fixed salary. An active family could well drown in comfort here.

But then Olle learned about the position, and he set heaven and earth in motion to get it, ran from Herod to Pilate to get references that could satisfy the appointing clerical authorities up here.

… They hear dogs baying from the wooded hillsides farther down in the valley, and there are tracks of reindeer herds everywhere. The reindeer have pawed up the snow and reveled in the copious and lovely iced reindeer moss[3] which there is the Lord's abundance of here in these parts.

But Jansa Olle knows in a month's time all the dog baying and all herder voices will be silenced in the entire inland – and he will have to be alone all the way to fall … well, I'll worry about that when the time comes.

They drive down the pine slope, down the last steep wooded hill and farther down the plain.

… And now Jansa Olle walks into the house, into his own house. He steps into the hallway that turns toward the north, looks into the room to the left – it looks rather deserted there –, then walks into the room on the right; here it is warm; it still smokes a little from dying embers in the fireplace, a candle in a bottleneck stands on the long table. The wood is nicely stacked at the side of the fireplace; the room has been cleaned and the floor strewn with evergreen branches. He walks into the small side room facing south; the bed in here is filled with soft birch twigs, and on the bed is spread a reindeer hide.

But he doeesn't find a living soul.

And yet he has obviously been expected. Curious, what these people can intend. And then to find the living room so clean and nice! That he hadn't expected.

The driver Bittoš Hansa unhitched the reindeer and headed out over the plain with them, in the direction they had heard barking dogs. He wanted to turn them loose in the herd there, so they could be well rested and eat themselves full before they headed back again tomorrow or the day after tomorrow.

---

[2] A placename with an original meaning of 'holy woods.'

[3] *Cladonia rangiferina*, also known as reindeer lichen.

Meanwhile, Olle emptied the sleds and carried his things inside, lit a fire in the fireplace and hung the kettle and coffeepot up. He found a key on the wall inside the small room, and in the storehouse lay flour and reindeer carcasses, – fancy reindeer coats and jackets were hanging on the walls; lassos and harnesses and driving reins of seal skin lay tossed on the floor. Some of the flour and salt belonged to him; that he, through an acquaintance of his down by the coast, had sent up here with some mountain Sámi who were visiting the market.

When Bittoš came back again the long table was set with steaming dishes, and they had a party. Olle had a half bottle of brandy in his trunk; but when Bittoš Hansa had asserted at the beginning of the trip he was devout and hadn't tasted liquor nor stolen reindeer for five years, he didn't dare take it out.

"I saw a couple of tents up there on the mountainside, but I didn't bother to go there; I just shouted to someone I saw outside that I released my reindeer in their herd, and that you had come."

"What did they say to that?"

"They asked what you looked like. Well, I said if you have ever seen an old Erik scared out of his wits, then you know roughly how Jansa Olle looks."

"And what are the people's names?"

"I don't know. But it is probably the ones who made it so clean and nice here in the house … She walks with her toes pointed out."

"Who?"

"Well, she who has done it. They are supposed to be such cleanly people these mountain Sámi who live in this parish. But there are not supposed to be many of them here in these tracts. Most of them live on the level mountain plateaus near the large settlement down there. But there are some of the West Parish's mountain Sámi too who have their camps here in the vicinity of Helligskogen. And you should take a trip up to the bordering folks, where the three kingdoms meet; it's just twenty miles up there. But to the Swedish church spot it is ninety miles, and a little farther to the Finnish by the big lake with the many hundreds of islands. Your father's parents came in their time from there, I know. They were able people; they all had dark eyes and black hair like you. But your mother was of the light, strong lineage – she had a high, narrow nose and a long, narrow face. Well, I've told you I've been down in your village, once in my youth."

Bittoš Hansa hadn't done much other in his life than driving. He had driven bishops and pastors and attorneys, fur buyers and Anabaptists and mystical refugees. He didn't entertain any superfluous respect for his people and didn't give a damn about unnecessary zeal to serve. But in spite of his quarrelsome nature, he had become an indispensible institution for all travelers up here. He had two worthless nags for pack horses for the summer and a few reindeer with threadbare hair for the winter trips. The man even had an aspect not to be trifled with, a cynically hanging face with gray, short, stiff stubble; his gray, watery eyes were terrifyingly round, and out of his ever open mouth stuck four colossal, lopsided teeth. Which race he belonged to, that our Lord may know.

But the West Parish's people, who accordingly didn't belong to this parish and this valley where the Helligskogen chapel was, were evidently a thorn in the eye for him. Yes, for Bittoš Hansa was originally a *Hoamm*á,[4] and *Hoammát* in a way can't stand people from the West Parishes.

"These folks from the West Parishes are blue-eyed and handsome enough, pure giants to look at. No one goes around as resplendently clad as they do when they are at markets and church grounds. Wide red and yellow and blue bands on caps and jackets, large silk kerchiefs around the neck, silver brooches on the belts and silver and pewter ornamentation on the sheaths. But at home they wear the same clothing, until the hair on the jacket and footwear falls off in large flakes, and a Christian man can't find lodging with them without getting vermin on himself. That comes from their not being believers. They are *bahkkinat*,[5] although they are baptized and have learned to read and acquired knowledge of God's word. They are given to drinking liquor, and they are loud and yoik like wild animals, steal reindeer and commit adultery at all times."

"That was a lot all at once," says Jansa Olle.

"Well, I'll never believe they are proper people" – and by people Bittoš Hansa really meant Sámi. "They're *stálut*,[6] who in the old days went astray in the mountains, and some have probably also come into being through adultery and other unchristian behavior. And for their sins God has punished them in the third and fourth generations. You saw that tent we lay in last night. It was a pure magpie's nest. If you see a decent sled or knife there, then one can swear they bought it from the East Parish."

"See a real person, a real reindeer Sámi! – he maintains good manners in his tent; everything is clean and nice, and all gentlemen say they can eat and sleep safely in his tent. He is devout and often trustworthy. He knows what is fitting for good people when one is at the market and in the church parish. I will not even speak about the settled Sámi down in your village. They are like settled people; it's just that they wear Sámi clothing; But their clothing is so fine, and they themselves are so excellent that the Sámi down by the sea and those on the mountain are just gnomes[7] in comparison."

*　　*
*

---

[4] *Hoamm*á, plural *Hoammát* – people from Kautokeino or the Western part of the Finnmark tundra.

[5] Heathens, from Late Latin *paganus*.

[6] Stallo – the steel-clad, an intruder of foreign origin.

[7] *Gufihttarat* (pl.) – gnomes, the hill folk or the subterranean ones.

Olle is lying on his bed in the small room – so he is lying again on a bed of birch twigs and reindeer hide. He has to lie with his right arm stretched straight out. The lameness in it had set in that dreadful night ...

Agnete had sent a message up to him a couple of times, while he lay in hospital, to ask whether he had anything against her coming to visit him. He had given the messenger the answer she could and she had to come. But both times she had stopped in the corridor and not come farther, and both times she had sent him the message afterwards that she had been prevented.

... So it should be, yes, so it should be. Should he maybe be alone in deciding how it should be. What was the paralysis in his arm, what was the bewitched, dark world that had been his existence during the crisis – yes, what did she have against that paralysis in his mind which she perhaps had gotten forever that night?

... There was a time he regarded every agony as an addition to the redeeming execution of the punishment on the verge of occurring – although he knew the execution would never happen, never could happen.

No, for he had committed a sin that was beyond ability.

Towards this sin her ability and desire to forgive had also been inadequate ... both times she had stopped in the corridor and had come no further – although she had then seen for herself he was sick.

And they would not meet later either. He hadn't seen her since that night. All the differences, also the divorce, had been arranged and dissolved through go-betweens and written negotiations.

On dances of sighing or mourning

They ate breakfast, and Olle now began to think about how he would adjust. The small room would be entirely his private sanctuary. The room with the fireplace and the room on the other side of the hall were for the 'common people,' when they showed up here for the holidays and otherwise.

And beyond his legally limited obligations as host he also had to do small favors for people. His permanent salary was three hundred crowns per year, and the idea was that the 'rest' he should get in tips – in the form of reindeer steaks, hides and such. The farseeing state had also built cow and hay barns, and if one has the accessories then one will always get the thing itself too. But who will milk the cows? No, the cow barn was probably simply a state supported signal to Olle; for what is a man with cows in the barn without women in the house? He is a pure and simple changeling.

… She walks with her toes pointed out … well, life in Helligskogen had drawn close to him; involuntarily he had to remember this oracular utterance of Bittoš Hansa yesterday evening.

Don't cross that bridge until you get to it, and he brushed aside that somewhat bold idea: … the man in a threadbare frock coat and with a large broad-brimmed felt hat on his head trudges away over a mountain plateau. The coattails flutter in the storm, and it starts to grow dark; but he tramps away with one shoulder lifted up toward the storm …

It is dead calm and a lovely March sun this morning, and Olle stands out in the yard and looks around. The house was without board siding and had a turf roof and was no higher than that an average horse could easily graze from the eaves.

The chapel which was a couple hundred steps from the house, farther in on the plain (this gift from God), had no board siding either, but the window frames were painted white, and the windows had doubled rounded arches. He was inside the chapel; both the pulpit and the altar piece with the carved cross were painted white, and there was sure enough also a little balcony above the entrance. And on the spot Olle posed the question to himself whether he too was allowed to mount the pulpit when he was going to read out loud the written meditation from the book of sermons about the day's text. Now with Easter approaching he was going to make his debut as a leader of devotions. Within the altar railing in any case he had nothing to do; that place was reserved for the holder of the holy minister's position down in the village when he visited Helligskogen once a year. And then Olle, Jansa Olle, the dentist Ole Janssen, the famous philosopher of aesthetics and ethics, the author of 'Cheerful Tenacity,' was going to officiate as sexton, – run after baptismal water, say the amen which somehow is not proper for a minister to say, and sing hymns at the top of his voice. Sure, why not? When the chief was honored, some of it could rub off on the sexton.

In a strange book he found in the small side room a Swede had written he had been here 'to saw lumber for the Lord's sanctuary.'

… Then Olle catches sight of a man driving over the plain; he is coming from the pine mountains farther north in the valley. The man is driving slowly and properly, clearly a decent and respectable man from the East Parish. Yes, for those from the West Parishe folks, as Bittoš Hansa said, run riot when they approach inhabited places; they holler aloud and yoik zealously – and how they drive! They can't even drive; they jerk to the left, throw the reins over the reindeer's back and jerk to the right, and their sled roads zigzag – wherever one comes across such a serpentine road, one can bet one's sweet life that it has been driven up by the West Parish folks.

Oh, Olle had suddenly become a full-blooded East Parish person again.

The man drives into the yard, slowly climbs out of the sled and looks at Olle – so, you have arrived – unties the reindeer and tethers it to a post below the storehouse. And now he walks over and takes him by the fist:

"But maybe you don't recognize me?"

"Yes, the face I remember to be sure, but –"

"Don't you remember Jauna Jauna[8] then?"

"Oh, damn, is it Jauna Jauna!" Olle positively jumped for joy.

"But you mustn't swear, old man. We are believers, many of us around here, and you are going to read God's word to us, you must remember."

"I beg your pardon. But it's so strange that … now when after twenty years' absence I am going to speak Sámi again, well then it's so easy for those improper words from boyhood days to come back without warning. I never swear in Norwegian, and besides I can consider myself as a believer, I too, in all humility anyway. And when you add goodwill then with God's help it can get better and better."

"Yes, that's true, he said … Well, you I remember well, Olle. But you turned into a decent man all the same I've heard people say … but why didn't you travel through your home village?"

Olle felt troubled by this question; he pleaded as an excuse his parents had, you know, died long ago, and for many reasons it felt more comfortable to take the shortcut over the West Parish.

---

[8] Jon's Jon, Jon Jonsen.

Jauna Jauna was a rather large fellow, and the thick reindeer jacket, which was raised up by a wide leather belt, made him loom even larger. His clear, dark blue eyes were surrounded by these distended fat pads that are often peculiar to well-nourished skippers – they probably come into being as a defense against windy weather – for the same reason blubber builds up on arctic animals. A thick, tarry stiff lasso, wound up in a ring, went over his right shoulder and under his left arm.

He took his sabre knife out of the sheath and banged and scraped the ice and snow from his feet. He undid the lacing at the front end of the sled and took up a black provision bag of dressed leather, got out some reindeer tongues and marrow bones – these shank knucklebones on the reindeer's back leg, whose marrow is so extraordinarily rich and thick inside the thin bone surface.

"Here I have a little welcome gift for you."

"Many thanks, Jauna Jauna."

"And in the storehouse I've put a reindeer carcass for you."

"You are …," Olle was on the verge of paying a little compliment, but checked himself, for Jauna Jauna would surely not suitably have appreciated being called a helluva guy or such.

They sat and drank coffee, and Olle happened to remember he had a half bottle of brandy in his bag. He went after it and asked Jauna Jauna whether there shouldn't be a little coffee and brandy.

"No, many thanks! Absolutely not! We don't use that stuff, no, thank heaven."

"Well, I'm not even asking you, Bittoš Hansa," and Olle went in again with the bottle.

But now Bittoš Hansa began to look out of the corner of his eye so oddly focusing on the bottle that stood on the table in the small room, stood there so golden red in the sun. He became more and more taciturn; it was as if he was drooling – finally said that he didn't feel good.

"You ought to lie down," Olle says.

"Yes … but I wondered whether a drop of brandy might not help."

"No, brandy never helps any illness," assured Jauna Jauna. "Some think so, of course, but it's just delusion and the devil's lies."

"In other words, you would gladly have had a nip, Bittoš Hansa," Olle says.

"No, not exactly a nip like that, but – a little as medicine."

But now Olle had noticed this development in his illness; it had both amused and irritated him, and it was with a lip smacking spite he said no – so as not to lead him into temptation, he said. And the remarkable thing was that Bittoš Hansa somehow had expected this answer, although Olle earlier had offered him a nip – and this moral setback had in advance brought about that he didn't get the right start when he tried to give vent to his resentment at being denied a nip, now that he really needed one.

It was a simple and villainous stroke of Olle; that, he acknowledged in silence also himself, but he had now tasted blood: Bittoš would get to carouse in this triple sin – first he would break a pledge of faith he had managed to hold for five years, and that by trying to lie his way to the nip, and now that he didn't get it, he found himself crestfallen in it like another worn out heavy drinker.

But now Bittoš Hansa was no worn out heavy drinker, in any case not anymore; when he had sat a while and struggled with the effect of this poisonous defeat, he got up suddenly and said:

"When I think about it, Olle, then I am glad you have refused me brandy. But I know you didn't do it out of respect for me – so I wouldn't get a taste for it –, you did it because you were coarse and malicious."

Olle felt inevitably struck down; – but pour him a nip, no, he wouldn't do that.

Bittoš Hansa dashed off in proud silence to fetch his reindeer he had released in Jauna Jaunas' herd yesterday evening.

Olle and Jauna Jauna still sat there; Bittoš Hansa's double-edged utterance had obviously caused them vexation. But then Jauna Jauna began to inquire about one thing or other from the wider world.

"… And around Kristiania there are probably not any reindeer Sámi, no. But there are supposed to be some on the high mountains to the south, I've heard. But they speak sort of another language than we. *Sare bárdni*,[9] who was down there a couple years ago, said he didn't understand them; he had to speak a settled person's language to them."

"But who has made it so nice and clean here in the house?" Olle asks.

"Well, that is my youngest daughter to be sure. Those winters she went to school down in the village she always lived with Erki Lemik Issak, and they are really nice and respectable Sámi farmers these people. Yes, I and my family always find lodging with Erki Lemik Issak when we are down in the village. Earlier on when the pasture was more copious on the level plateaus down there and we could stay in those tracts during the winter, we were often down in the village; we were there both Christmas and Easter, and when there were judicial assembly meetings in the village. Then it was often grand down there. People dressed up came from distant regions, from the fjords and from Finland and river people from far within. I remember we once at the same time had a visit of the bishop and district governor and bailiff and two attorneys and a dean. And at that time the merchant still had the right to sell brandy, and we then often stood at the counter and drank half-pint shots we paid for with reindeer steaks and reindeer tongues. Yeah, for an unconverted person which I too was at that time, it could often be quite fun in those seasons … when one isn't thinking about one's immortal soul's salvation. That's for sure … It was really nice this tobacco."

"Yes, now we'll have Easter soon, Olle, and then there will be a celebration here in Helligskogen. People will hear you have come, and then they will come down

9 Sara's son.

here, those who think it is too far to travel down to the villages … Here in Hellig-skogen people sacrificed in the old days to strange gods, and *noaidit*[10] yoiked un-godly songs until they became deranged, fell over and saw visions, and many of them performed unchristian miracles, some for good, others for evil."

… Jauna Jauna and Olle hadn't sat and talked to each other for more than a couple hours when Bittoš Hansa appeared in the yard with his reindeer. He came in in a hurry, and even before he managed to close the door after himself, he started to storm away – his gall must have increased quite significantly in the meanwhile.

"Let me have the money you owe me."

Olle paid him the hundred crowns and handed him besides a ten spot as a tip. But Bittoš Hansa threw the ten spot on the table:

"It's only from prominent men I accept tips. A mountain hostel host shouldn't pretend to be a big shot. You are hired here to wash the floor, fetch water and chop wood for the mountain Sámi, and you are going to live by accepting tips from peo-ple … No, the devil should have to deal with such people as you!"

Jauna Jauna got up angry and appalled:

"And you call yourself a believer!"

"I … no," Bittoš Hansa answered like a beast, went out and hitched up the rein-deer. Olle and Jauna Jauna stood outside in the yard and tried to talk sense into him. Bittoš Hansa didn't even take the trouble to reply; he ran in to get his provision bag, – he came inevitably to look into the small room; the bottle still stood on the table, and without for a moment thinking it over he put it down in the bag. And at the next moment Bittoš Hansa was off.

And while the two stand there and watch him drive over the plain at a furious pace, Olle suddenly is struck by a hunch … yes, quite right! Olle comes rushing out:

"Lend me your reindeer! The Bittoš devil has stolen the flask. I don't give a damn about the brandy; but he shall in any case not have it!"

Jauna Jauna got so excited that he simply forgot to warn Olle against swearing.

Olle drove away as he stood and walked, bareheaded and with only a jacket. The snow flew, and the reindeer started off as if it was itself the offended and stolen … it panted heavily up over the wooded hills, and while Bittoš Hansa sits in the sled and hammers with his bare knuckles on the bottom of the flask to drive out the cork, a reindeer rushes up past his string – he gives a start so the flask falls from his hand.

"You damned brandy thief!" And Olle seizes the flask. "Now I cheated you good, you apostate wretch and thief!" But now it flared up in Bittoš Hansa too, and before they realized it, they fell into the wildest fight; the reindeer were scared out of their wits, and the whole string and Olle's reindeer too were clustered together; finally, the two brawlers were also entangled in the cluster. At last, they both became so dog-tired that they were hardly able to breathe, and Olle who began to fear he would lose, used his last strength to hit the flask against a sled. And when Bittoš Hansa

---

[10] *Noaidi*, pl. *noaiddit* – shaman and/or medicine man.

heard the fatal splashing sound, he stopped as if stunned and remained on his knees staring at this ruin of bits of broken flask and the yellowish moist spot in the snow. He resolutely got prone over the spot and slurped into himself the brandy saturated slush.

Olle broke into laughter, he laughed so much he became sore, couldn't manage anything more, just laughed; he made a generous gesture of hospitality:

"Well, please, good sir, drink to your heart's desire!"

Bittoš Hansa didn't say a word; he sucked the snow slush down to the bluest ice. His sense of shame had gone the same way as this liquid of conflict; he literally drank himself down into the snow; he lay with his entire upper body down on the ground. Finally, he got up; the hard-earned brandy had made him almost gentle; he said with a silly expression:

"No, you duped me all the same."

"But now you have eaten and drunk yourself to destruction."

"Let me be!"

"Let you be! You'll go to hell. You have been abstinent and devout for five years, but now for the sake of the miserable brandy made yourself both a thief and drunkard and atheist. You have sinned against the very Holy Ghost, and for that sin there is no forgiveness, you know."

"Oh, I'll surely manage to do penance for this. And the whole thing is your fault. Had you been a true gentleman you would have offered me a nip at the same time as you offered one to Jauna Jauna. And I would then have said no thanks and been glad that I said no thanks. But it was your pitiful act that aroused the evil spirits in me. You are the most wretched coward I have met in my life. Farewell, scoundrel."

And Bittoš Hansa drove off.

… The good man of God Jauna Jauna laughed sinfully unrestrained when Olle told him the episode. But right after, he regretted it and said some nice words about God and sin and Bittoš Hansa.

He asked Olle to come and visit him and his family; the camp lay up on the mountainside, barely three miles from here. And then drove home.

On reindeer

And now Olle is alone. But he doesn't feel any of the insidious anxiety that had so often been his only company the past two years when he sat alone at home and tried to put off the unpleasant guest with an assurance that fate is fate.

... The river that runs past here, through Helligskogen's valley, also runs through the village down there ...

Olle was no older than four-five years when he 'astonished the world' with his exceptional ability to ring the bell in the schoolhouse tower. The long rope swung rhythmically and steadily so the bell in the tower became perfectly elated and oscillated festively and solemnly like a church bell; one would never have believed there was such a full sounding brass ring in that tattered bell. People had him ring, and the boy could get so wrapped up in it he felt hot and cold shudders rush through himself.

But throughout his boyhood years he became a symbol of contradiction in the village – oh, Olle couldn't help it he didn't have time to calculate the consequences of his actions; the actions always took him in their power. If he drove to the mountains to get reindeer moss or up the river for a load of hay from one of the hayfields, he tried to promise God and himself he would drive nicely; but when he came back the horse was sweaty, and he had to sneak it into the stall so his father wouldn't find out about it.

As far back as he could remember it had happened to him now and then he had been attacked by something he himself and others thought were headaches ... no, every time later in life he remembered these attacks from the strange forces on a poor little, innocent person, then he knew it couldn't be characterized as a common, proper headache ... no, it was a break-in from a hidden world; one or other place there must have been a fissure in his consciousness, in his nervous system, and he was without mercy put face to face with the terrible, which are the open entrances toward that place only God can see without having to invoke help in the stress of confusion ... Even today he could remember how he once had seen the frightfully large sun go, actually leave ... he himself walked on his hands, and walking on his hands he was going to reach the sun – an obscure riddle of an impossibility he was condemned to conquer.

The attacks had stopped in his fourteenth year. Much, much later, during a certain period of his life, he would also get to experience existence in another abyss … dream life in Hades' shadow kingdom.

No, my fate is not my fate! It is the enemy I am condemned to fight against … a crafty and indefatigable bird Phoenix of an enemy, with this capricious ability to transform itself into something completely unrecognizable … as a rule I don't know it is him; I think I'm dealing with a friend; he arranges everything to the best for me, heaps surprises on me that make me drunk with ecstasy.

… Olle lies awake on his good birch twig mattress in the small room, with his lame hand stretched straight out … What if Agnete knocked on the window now? And he asks himself a question that hadn't occurred before, but that now gets him to start up: would he, when all is said and done, be able to close the door on her now? – wouldn't he also now as that time be possessed by 'Cheerful Tenacity?'

He stands at the window, and in the moonlight he sees a fox moving with small jerks to the side over the snow-covered ice on the river and disappear into the birch scrub beneath the bare, round mountain over there on the other side … No, my fate isn't my fate; it is just a deceptively crafty shadow moving and sneaking up on me.

* *
*

Olle had eaten breakfast and was enjoying a pipe of tobacco. He had already begun to feel at home little by little.

There was sunshine and calm weather too this morning, and now he got an uncontrollable desire to visit Jauna Jauna's camp up on the mountainside.

He goes on skis over the plain, this God's gift of an open plain, that protects the mind against the depressing feeling one gets from having the forest and the mountainsides hanging over one nearby.

He goes up the first, steep wooded hill and follows the sled road across a flat pine barren. Here the snow has been tramped down by reindeer everywhere – in places one can walk as on a firm main road. And the grazing reindeer herds have dug a countless number of holes in the masses of snow. They can smell where there is a patch of moss under a couple yards of deep snow, and they immediately kick up a hole as they dive with the whole front part of the body and stretch forward so the snow piles up on both sides like the spray around the bow. And the lovely ice-fresh, greenish white reindeer moss is also worth this all-out effort.

Olle heads up the first mountainous hillside; here the pine forest is sparser, and the sun-illuminated patches on the forest floor become larger. He hears human voices and dogs barking. Then he glimpses between the tree trunks a couple smoky tents on an open spot in the woods. The dogs have still not picked up his scent – fortunately, he is in Sámi raingear; the animals, in any case, don't need to take him to be a _stallo_.[11] But he stops anyway involuntarily and remains standing for a while.

---

[11] In Sámi folklore, a human-like creature who eats people.

The tent poles stick up blue-black from the smoke hole. Sleds lie overturned outside, and on the trees around hang clothing and bedclothes and pieces of meat, kettles, pots, harnesses, lassos and whatever. A woman comes walking out of the grove. A couple dogs slip out of the tent, look around, sniff a little at the sleds and one thing and another and then go in again.

It looks so very domestic, the whole thing.

At the next moment the pack of dogs comes out of both tents, a hell of an animal howl fills the air, and Olle's eyes grow dim when he takes fate in his hands and walks toward this inundation of barking rows of teeth. And in his distress he bellows out in the dogs' own mother tongue: he curses them with a selection of the reindeer Sámi's best dog oaths. And the dogs seemed to be satisfied with it: when a man speaks so respectably and openly, well … they must at least try to let him come forth alive.

And now Jauna Jaunas' family stood out in the 'yard' and welcomed Olle with the most delightful and the most genuine smiles.

Yes, he then found out little by little she there was his wife, and this one here – yes, this is my youngest daughter; she is the one who has tried to put things in order a little down there where you came. And the one there is my married daughter, and that is her husband – and their children – they live in that tent there.

"And where is the herd?"

"It's farther north on the wooded hillsides. There is such good pasture there."

Olle got such an immediately charming impression of this family that he felt it as a great happiness he had gotten these people as neighbors. He didn't have time now to think that in a month's time or so they would move up to the peninsulas way to the north, and he wouldn't see them again until well into the fall … Perhaps they wouldn't come back to these parts again at all.

And while they stood there and exchanged the first halting words, he was in a way not able to take his eyes off Aile, the youngest daughter – such a young girl with golden hair and blue eyes in a Sámi costume is already in itself a provocative sight – and then to meet this sight up here … No, Olle willing or unwilling had to allow the illusions to knock about.

And the one who didn't take long to notice it was Gudnel, the married daughter – my God, how she looked so fervently in a good mood and cheerful! All young, plump, pretty women are splendid down to the cockles of their hearts. Olle had an instinctive hunch she could become an equally influential as willing protector and advisor to him. Oh, how he needed someone who could look after his well-being! No, such a married sister who is even pretty and young and plump and cheerful – she is a pure gift from God.

And the old one – she really looked like a mistress of the house 'of the good, old school.' In her elaborate belt, woven of multicolored warp threads, hung keys and a needlehouse of brass and a knife whose pewter fitted shaft stuck up from an elegantly carved sheath of reindeer antler. In contrast to the daughters she was rather

Asiatic looking, had this sharp radiance in her coal black pupils, and it sparkled so distant under the long, heavy eyelids – perhaps the somewhat flattened face made it look wider than it actually was.

"Well, who would have believed we should get you as the host here in Helligskogen, says the old one, Mother Jauna. But it's probably not just to be host you have come here, you have other things to do," – and a little, friendly sly smile sparkled in her dry, wrinkled face.

Indeed, the old one knew what she was going to say. Olle wasn't the prodigal son who had had to be thankful to be a host for a few Sámi souls, and that even outside the Sámi's own civilization. No, he had other things to do. And this was in reality the first edifying greeting Olle had gotten. If the rest of the congregation also considered him and his position from that standpoint, then much would have been won. He would be spared from explaining himself – a hint of mystery would be a great help in one or other situation.

"You may go in then," says Jauna Jauna.

The heather floor was covered with birch twigs, and reindeer hides and jackets lay around the hearth over which a huge kettle hung – it hangs and boils there from the time the tent is put up until it is taken down again. Uppermost were coffeepots and food bags and wooden dishes and cups and other utensils.

Mother Jauna stuck a couple reindeer tongues, some marrow bones and various delicious pieces of meat up in the kettle, and Aile tended the coffeepot. You know, there was company here. And Olle had with him a cram-full pouch with extra fine tobacco. Aile went out after reindeer cheese and a 'stomach' with frozen reindeer milk – it was like the purest ice cream. Reindeer milk you see is extraordinarily fat, doubly as fat as goat milk; in the summer, cheese is made out of it; in the autumn they freeze it in an inside-out reindeer stomach, and it can be preserved fresh the entire winter.

Then they ate and drank a prodigious amount of coffee – good heavens, how a pipe of tobacco tasted good afterwards!

"But how are you going to manage without a wife here in Helligskogen?" asks Gudnel, the young, married, plump angel.

Oh, how they laughed!

"Well, say it, Gudnel! I hope you will aid me in finding a remedy."

"But haven't you been married?" asks the old one.

And now Olle had to swallow a bitter pill to say he was divorced – they couldn't get along with each other, and so there was nothing else to do but divorce. But he understood right away they knew this chapter. That a man and woman can live like dog and cat together, can't be helped, as is known; but to divorce for that reason – only they do that who otherwise also become objects of public ridicule by proper people; but otherwise there has not been a divorce at all in these tracts. Not to mention infidelity – certainly they have heard that sort of thing occurs with the licentious among Norwegian big shots; but it is perceived as so distant and shudderingly daring that the reality and difference between good and evil is somehow erased.

But when the Jauna Jaunas otherwise set store by Olle and invariably thought the best of him, then they would in any case believe it had just been bad temper on her part that had been the undoing.

"But you two could of course be reconciled again," Gudnel tried anew.

"No, certainly not; they were legally divorced, and if they were to get together again they would have to remarry."

"We were thinking about traveling down to the village at Easter, some of us," Mother Jauna says. "But since you have come now and there'll be an Easter celebration here, then it would be almost finer to be here, in any case for us old ones. Yes, for these young folks will perhaps travel down anyway."

"No, we're staying here," says Gudnel. "Aile will have to travel alone."

"Is that so," Olle said, and it was as if something bad bunched up in his chest. "Aile must absolutely do down to the village. Well, I understand."

For, good grief, he thought, it was just as well to resign himself to it the sooner the better.

"No, do you think I want to travel alone," Aile says and looks at Gudnel.

"Maybe Erki Lemik Issak has a son," Olle says and tries to be cheerful.

"Yes, he has," Gudnel says and doesn't let herself be restrained at all by Aile's angry glance. "And it's really one of these hidebound village show-offs who always go around in fancy clothes," – Gudnel feels completely at home. "All the village people who have married daughters of mountain Sámi have gotten rich."

"Yeah, that's true," Olle says. "Have a farmstead and horse and cows and sheep and a herd of reindeer with their parents-in-law in the mountains; that's something. Look for example at Nilas Hansa. Money in the bank, cellar full of salmon and storehouse full of everything imaginable. And drives mail and drives big shots all winter. Can a person wish to have it better?"

"Well, not for that, I wouldn't swap," says Gudnel and pats her little, thin and swarthy husband on the back. She could well have him on her lap, and he would sit there and, with his innocent little eyes, look at her motherly good face. Yes, for a woman can also understand that sort of love for a man.

Little-Andi as he was also called by the family glowed too with filial confidence. Gudnel was his good guardian; every little affront to him was an affront to her, and if he wasn't in a position to defend himself, then by the living God she was. And who knows – maybe he was a whiz as a lover, when it counted – such small, slender little things one can't always weigh by the simple earthly weight.

"Do you know the Kristiania *ámtamánni* (administrative officer)?" asks Jauna Jauna.

"No."

"But you've lived in Kristiania."

"Yes, I have to be sure; but it doesn't follow that everyone gets to the Kristiania administrative officer."

"No no, that's true for sure. It is probably only the very finest big wigs that get there. He is supposed to be the greatest legally trained man in the country, I've heard. He knows the laws both in England and France – and laws that people had thousands of years ago, and that were written on leather and stone."

But Little-Andi backed the Bergen administrative officer who didn't dread putting on oilskins and personally going to sea to better be able to write a law for seamen.

Then they were very busy talking about the Saivo family which was supposed to live just five miles or so to the west, and it dawned on Olle that the Saivo family was the pure exception among the West Parish folks; they didn't steal reindeer, they were believers, they didn't commit adultery, and they didn't drink brandy. Jauna Jauna was genuinely delighted there really were such people among the West Parish folks. It was as if there weren't other honorable people in the world than the Saivo family.

And now Gudnel couldn't contain herself any longer, – she sat and talked about Saivo Piera, the son in this marvelous family, and Olle, whose senses had gotten so eagerly attentive at the sight of Aile, could clearly understand that Saivo Piera was dedicated a quite different serious and cautious mention than Erki Lemik Issak's son down in the east village.

He tried to take comfort that one could not expect a young girl like Aile to be without a suitor; but that comfort didn't sit well against the background that he himself was forty-two years old.

But now one of the herders comes and tells the following shocking story.

This morning he had become aware of a flock of ravens flying and flapping above the wooded slope to the west. They shrieked and made a row, and new flocks came flying from all directions.

There must have been a dead reindeer lying there, he thought, and he headed up there on skis. He had a feeling of something unpleasant, while he was going up there – what it was he didn't know, but there is always something unpleasant with these blue black, gloom-boding beings in the air – their shrieks and ragged wings always seem to circle around something dismal.

Then he gets to the raven lair; it is like a pure Doomsday; he has to shriek and flap his arms to frighten the ravens a little away. And then he catches sight of a rolled up heap of reindeer jacket lying on the sled road. It was Bittoš Hansa. He was dead.

That whole quantity of snow slush the brandy had tempted him to slurp into himself had been too much for his stomach and intestines.

Bittoš Hansa's reindeer and sleds were later found farther up, right by the timberline. The animals were then worn down by hunger; they had gotten tied up and couldn't move from the spot to find pasture.

The herder was sent away the following day with Bittoš Hansa's earthly remains and his reindeer and sleds. He was going to drive the body to the West Parish's church grounds so it could be buried there. Driving with it all the way down to the sea district where Bittoš Hansa was from, Jauna Jauna thought, was absolutely meaningless; in any case, the West Parish folks had to do it if they didn't want to bury him there.

Here in Helligskogen the graveyard had not yet been consecrated. People had not had a chance to think about the dead when the chapel was consecrated as a house of God last fall.

The herder took along with him a written account of Bittoš Hansa's tragic death.

On the usefulness of this animal

A person's death in the wilderness is already in itself a serious occurrence. And besides Bittoš Hansa's death was aurrounded by all the desolate atmosphere that had mounted up around him the last day he was alive.

Olle had to acknowledge that his conduct toward the deceased had been mean, and it had been the direct cause of the end. Now he himself had related he had been in a fight with Bittoš Hansa, and it wasn't precluded that he too could be suspected of murder.

Olle plods around alone in the rooms.

And then this with Aile. If he doesn't come there, older male, and imagine he has stepped into a virginal Paradise where a young Eve goes into raptures at this revelation: – there is the man I have dreamt about! And of course he assumed the angel Gudnel's only happiness consisted of bringing the two together.

… It was true Agnete had been in the hospital's corridor, but it was also true she had stopped in the corridor and not gone into him. It was supposed to be like that, yes, It was supposed to be like that.

And when they had settled their last differences through the lawyer, and all danger like that was eliminated, he had through a common acquaintance asked her for a final and only conversation. No, she had nothing to talk about with him. It was supposed to be like that.

But now it happens for the first time that Olle questions himself whether this really was such an unforgivable sin to say to a wife who had fled, who in the middle of the night knocks on the window of her abandoned husband's place, she had surely been in the wrong – she didn't live there.

And Olle reads a couple chapters in 'Cheerful Tenacity' before he goes to bed.

No, my fate is not my fate. It is only my evil, dismal shadow that can hit on playing tricks with yellow slush – not to punish Bittoš Hansa – the one who dies doesn't suffer evil from dying – but to fan myself on the nose with the reflection from the confounded world.

I no longer acknowledge my fate and will not allow myself to be browbeaten by its pranks. I've become a grown man now.

And Olle reads one more chapter in 'Cheerful Tenacity.'

Easter didn't come this year until well into April

And now Holy Week had arrived. Olle had felled some birch trees on a little headland farther up – where the two rivers meet. He had also felled a couple bare pines up on the wooded hillside – properly, of these old men of the forest turned gray long ago that have shed all their bark, and whose shriveled, naked branches bristle out. They are just waiting for the roots in a generation or so to be chafed enough by perishability that an autumn storm can give them the last coup de grace and let the earth get its own back.

The axe blows sang in the forest day after day, and Jauna Jauna was of assistance in bringing the wood out. They used four reindeer for that; for it isn't much a sled can hold and a single reindeer can pull; but otherwise Jauna Jauna thought it was ludicrous to struggle so much with this wood; but he finally lost his patience, from pure irritation at such unreasonableness. Couldn't Olle like other folks fetch wood from the forest little by little, depending on his need.

He had had a visit from people from other and more distant Sámi villages than Jauna Jauna's. So now people in the reindeer villages on the mountain plateaus and in the valleys knew the host and prayer leader had arrived. He would get a full house for Easter.

All of Jauna Jauna's people had been here too, and Aile and Gudnel and the old one had been seriously busy going over his things: clothing, toiletries, books, fishing equipment, revolver, rifle, tools and such. He even had to get out his underwear, and the sight of a pair of violet tricot underpants got them to fall silent with solemn delight. Olle had even taken along a frock coat too; for it might happen he would go to a merchant's party in one of the villages, and he didn't want to be a poorer fellow than the minister and sexton and sheriff. That much they knew!

… Olle had become miraculously healthy and new at this time. When all is said and done, it is a mere trifle to be happy, and yet one can for an entire generation go and turn upside down to try to get hold of a happiness one actually has in one's pocket.

His previously so very nice casual clothes had become rather dingy from work. And in the evenings he sat big and in command and tired, assessed the day's work and made plans.

Wednesday before Maundy Thursday Aile came down to spend Easter here and be his right hand. He joked crudely and spoke impartially to her and was anything but a suitor and Don Juan; one has to behave like people to people – if one is to get anywhere with them.

Olle stands in the yard and is shaping a sled runner, and Aile is on her way to the storehouse; she stops on the steps and listens.

"I hear bells," she shouts to him. "Aren't you going to ring in the church holiday then?"

"Oh, you are really right about that! If there is going to be a holiday, then there is going to be a holiday. And I'm going to ring so Helligskogen will know it."

And Olle hurries over to the chapel. He rings and rings, and the little bell swings in time up there in the steeple on 'the Lord's temple,' the good Swedish man had 'sågat timmer till.'[12] He hadn't forgotten the art from his childhood; he could still make people happy with festive bell sounds. And he goes up in the steeple and repeatedly rings and beats every so often the three slow beats.

… Over the level mountain plateaus from the valley come festively clad people driving down toward Helligskogen. The red and yellow and blue finery on the jackets and harnesses are greatly resplendent against the snow. All the way from the highest mountain cliffs they can see the chapel. And now the one in front stops; he climbs out of the sled and shouts to those behind:

"See, there we have our church! Can you hear the bells ringing? That's probably Olle who's ringing in the Easter holiday."

And with their hearts filled with holiday joy they drive on down the wooded mountain slope. From a steep mountain slope with sparse woods they catch sight of others driving down both valleys above – presumably people from the Finnish and Swedish border districts. And others come up the ice on the river below, the East Parish people, the local people here in these neighborhoods.

… Olle rings and chimes repeatedly; there is nothing to save for; everyone from the mountains and valley will get their welcome greeting, and he knows so very well how it warms their hearts to get to hear the sound of the church bell.

The yard was teeming with people and reindeer and sleds and dogs when he came back from the chapel. And more were on the way – this desolate and endlessly big wilderness was nevertheless really full of people when it came right down to it.

Year after year they meet off and on, at a market, in a village, along a main road on the plateau or in a valley, or in the summer quarters on one of the long peninsulas far to the north. Or when they take a trip over to the neighboring reindeer camps to look for lost reindeer.

And at the bonfire in the strange tent on the mountain somewhere they then have news to tell, – yes, my God, how nice it is to hear news – who has gotten married there, how many reindeer Sammulaš is said to have, who has been convicted of reindeer theft – to hear about remarkable events in the wider world and about signs seen in the sky.

… An old man comes and takes Olle by the hand, glances at the others and says with an extraordinaryly sonorous voice:

"We welcome you, Jansa Olle, and may God bless you and your work here!"

And the little, pithy welcome speech made an impression both on Olle and on the others; it was an immediate reminder that Olle's position really was significant – at least it could become so if he had the right urge to bring it about. And he believed

---

[12] Swedish for 'sawed lumber for.'

and hoped so himself that he had. He walked around with a certain clerical dignity and shook everyone's hand as it says. *Buorre beaivi – Ipmil atti*[13] was heard constantly. But Aile seemed to awaken an even greater attention than Olle, – oh, her blond golden hair and this face, her walking, posture, attire!

"She is just like *gusavuodja*,"[14] whispered a thunderstruck old woman as Aile walked past. It was as seriously meant as it was seriously construed. Can a mountain Sámi imagine anything more delicious than *gusavuodja*. And then Aile kept this pet name; she felt flattered, and expert yoikers immediately made a yoik in her honor:

> *Gusavuodja, gusavuodja,*
> la li lo lo, la la la la
> wealth, finery and hair like gold,
> *gusavuodja, gusavuodja.*

The resounding, red splotched mounds of jackets flowed together, flowed around during the busily changing handshakes, and the voices sounded affectionate and they shrieked with ecstasy:

"Is that really Little-Andi? And you are his wife? Well, I've heard about you, Gudnel." — "Wolves? – No, not since last year." "Yes, we are exalted, we too, yes, thanks and praise to the Lord; it's blessed to believe. And how is *Mákká gánda*?"[15]

The dogs went around and greeted and sniffed each other, rushed into fights, shaggy, yelping balls rolled between people's legs who also raised their angry voices and kicked and scolded and swore as if Easter and faith and Christian life didn't exist on earth any longer.

Helligskogen's large state church kettle which Aile and Olle ahead of time had hung over the fireplace hearth in the large room was filled quickly with marked pieces of meat – they also had to use the kettle in the cow barn passage. And Olle carried water and wood and was on the go everywhere. A more open host they couldn't wish for. And then he was Jansa Olle, he who could make silver teeth, and teeth with which one could grind pot shards into wheat flour.

The Jauna Jaunas had also arrived here this afternoon, and Gudnel and the old one had taken a spot on the storehouse steps – there they could keep an eye on everything and everyone.

"Look there are *Anáračču*,"[16] and Gudnel nudged her mother with her elbow, "and there are the Swedish knit caps."

Anáračču were definitely the genuine small parched, those with the broad, yellow and flat faces who were not at all Chinese. Oh, how they were owl-like soundless in their movements – so sneakily unobtrusive where they ambled around, bow-legged and pigeon-toed, and fiddled with their sleds and food sacks. They took up

---

[13] Hello – may God grant!

[14] *Gusavuodja* – cow butter.

[15] *Mákká gánda*, Magga's boy.

[16] *Anáračču* (pl.) – people from the Finnish bordering parish.

so little room at the hearth, on the floor, out in the yard; they were never in the way of anyone. And when well into the night they readied a bed on the floor in the large room and changed footwear and the soft as silk pounded sedge,[17] the Sámi use instead of stockings, their feet were as white and clean and full-sized as Adam's and Eve's were before the fall. They always found something to hang footware up on to dry, and the sedge they put behind the headboard, a rolled up jacket – thank heavens there is enough space in this world. Yes, these people would probably know how to manage in all kinds of autumn rain and dreary weather. To this very day untouched by this world – they had hardly ever seen the ocean, some of them – they were virtually thought of as arctic people from the hand of the maker on. Their oval boxes of thin, whole birch sheets, their sheaths, their food bowls from the large growths on the birch – the burls, their sleds and harnesses and such – all small works of art. Yes, how the one bowl and the one sled had to have occupied their eye and mind, while they worked on it during the winter and continued to work on it over the summer.

Mother Jauna and Gudnel had it nice where they sat on the storehouse steps. Here showed up a really sensational number of young men – many of them even perhaps would have had a shorter or in any case more convenient way down to their respective villages than here to Helligskogen. For if they didn't know Aile in another way, then they in any case had heard her spoken of. Many a song had been yoiked in her honor on the calm moonlit nights, while this or that young person had been guarding the reindeer herd and, undisturbed by the wolves, could devote himself to his dream about Aile or another *gusavuodja*.

It was to be sure a poor consolation Olle had to deal with; but still it was a consolation. He had restrained himself towards Aile with praiseworthy energy, and now it benefited him. It would have looked pretty if he, Jansa Olle, would have made his debut here as a fool before all the people.

But all of a sudden it gets quiet in the yard; everyone's eyes are directed toward the wooded slope to the west where a noisy bell sound is heard. And a little later a festively clad retinue is seen coming driving at full speed, at a gallop, down the last, steep mountainside hill and further across the plain. They are yoiking at full voice, the one in front driving with a snowwhite reindeer; harness and bell collar are resplendent in red and yellow and blue. And he himself is also in a snowwhite jacket whose high collar is decorated with a broad band of scarlet cloth that runs out in two long, fluttering bows, – he is on one knee in the sled with the left one waving outside, whoa! how he cracks the whip, while the other arm chops urging in the air and the large four-sided and red crown of his cap dances like fire in a storm. The rein swings constantly over the back of the reindeer; he jerks first to the one side, then to the other – and the animal runs at a zigzag as if it were right in the middle of a desperate running of the gantlet … well, by the living God, that's how the West

---

[17] *Carex vesicaria.*

Parish folks drive, always in a zigzag, and that is how they always come driving into the village – festively and flamboyantly.

It was the Saivo family, with Saivo Piera at the head. The other West Parish people had come earlier.

Oh, they had probably intended it, the Saivos, – they would have the whole gathering as admiring spectators – there come the Saivos … People and dogs swept themselves out of the way just as Saivo Piera's reindeer with noisy lungs, with tongue trembling out of its mouth and with streams of breath out of its nostrils came dashing in and turned sharply so the snarling sled swept over the hard-packed snow in the yard.

Saivo Piera leapt up, big and tall and with the West Parish's blue-eyed hawk aspect inflamed by the speed and seriousness of the moment – everyone knew that this was more than an Easter trip for the Saivos … and from the moment people became aware of the bell sound on the mountainside, Aile had become busier with her hostess duties than ever, – poor little, fair Aile! – she of course had to see to calming her heartbeat more or less. For such a retinue must always cause a girl's heart to beat, – whatever might otherwise be wrong with the same girl's heart.

Olle couldn't help it; he felt it tighten quite unpleasantly and bad in his chest and head. For it was that very Saivo Piera Gudnel had spoken about the first time he visited the Jauna Jaunas up on the mountainside.

But one of the group came driving slowly after – it was old father Saivo – the hallowed miracle among the West Parish folks who had become renowned and almost a hallowed saint because he, the West Parish man, didn't steal reindeer and didn't drink brandy, led devotions in his tent and was on the whole what one calls an honorable man.

The company unhitched their reindeer, and one person went with them up onto the wooded slope to turn them loose in Jauna Jauna's herd – which also those who came earlier had done. There the animals could graze at Easter, while the people themselves were here reveling in the friendly atmosphere and the turf hut and the word of God and hymns.

Old Saivo looked around – his eyelids were long and sharply angled – and then he said as if blessing:

"*Buorre beaivi ja Ipmil ráfi buohkat!*"[18]

And he walked around and greeted people as the miracle he was and felt himself to be. The other West Parish folks looked at him and each other with radiant smiles, at the East Parish folks, *Anáračču* and the Swedish with the knit caps; it was as if they wanted to say: "Yes, there you see him, old Saivo!" It was claimed even the most light-fingered West Parish folks shrunk from stealing reindeer that had Saivo's earmark: the three cuts on the front edge of the left ear. And when there was an assembly meeting over in their own village, a half dozen reindeer thieves who were at the

---

[18] Hello and God's peace to everyone!

moment under indictment could sit in a ring on their sleds in a yard and shed tears of enthusiasm for old Saivo, while the bottle went around: his equal as an honorable old person didn't exist! And if anyone would claim he was just as good as Saivo then he could go where the pepper grows with such shameless bragging.

And also the East Parish people and the *Anáraččat* and the Swedish with the knit caps with whom it was not so uncommon to be an honorable person, felt involuntarily dazzled when they stood face to face with this saint.

When the old village chieftain in the East Parish who had drained the West Parish of several rich tax objects, also wanted to lure Saivo into moving over, the West Parish's township board beseeched Saivo not to abandon them – not so much for the sake of the pitiable money; but they couldn't afford to get rid of him themselves.

Gudnel and the old one still had it ticklingly happy where they were sitting on the storehouse steps – most excitedly they poked each other every time they caught sight of Olle – how he was going to take this, that was the question that got the roots of their hearts to squirm with excitement. Gudnel's face could assume the most distorted shapes from curiosity alone; it was as if she had an inflamed ear itch.

The Saivos said hello to the Jauna Jaunas very meaningfully, and Saivo Piera immediately tried to stop the ceaselessly scurrying Aile; but she dashed around like a helpless feather in a whirlwind; she seemed to have abandoned herself unconditionally to motion.

… But how these West Parish folks stood out from all the others! – So tall and strapping in shape, so blue-eyed and pure lined in coountenance. And then all that resplendent finery, and these gorgeous voices! When they talked, they spoke in the style of the old sagas, slowly and dignified – if they cursed or scolded a dog, then it sounded like a sermon in a loftier style.

But if one examined the finery and all the rest more closely … oh, good grief, the East Parish folks had to laugh at such, – although there was a little envy concealed in it; for both the finery and the West Parish folks impressed them in spite of everything.

Here wealthy Saivo Piera walked around in a jacket as shapeless as it was stiff – they couldn't treat the hide! – with a neck much too open and a collar too high, decorated with yellow and red and blue pieces of cloth in zigzag. And sinew thread stuck out on the outerside of the seams – on the hair side – may God forgive an East Parish old woman! She had to be amazed at such a sight. The stiff, shapeless jacket was hitched up with a colossally wide leather belt from which all sorts of bangles of copper and brass and steel hung. And then the cap, with the four-sided crown of red cloth which otherwise was of ordinary reindeer calfskin and besides sewed together from square-shaped patches of hide of different hair colors; that should somehow be more beautiful! – oh, good grief Jeremiah! – if a dandy of an East Parisher would show up in such … absolutely never would he show up in such, he, whose winter cap was always of the darkest and finest otterskin, with a fine little edge of white reindeer calfskin, and the square crown was always of black cloth. And then the bellings[19] and footwear on Saivo Piera! – the one who had a large herd to take care of … an ordinary Sámi farmer in the East Parish who would have to buy all that, he wears bellings sewed together from the blackest and most densely haired parts of the hide on the reindeer's legs, but also his footwear is like a little ballad.

But Saivo Piera and all the other West Parish folks nevertheless acted with an attitude as if they constituted a general staff. And they were that way too at home in magpie nests of tents on the West Parish's plateaus and mountains. The hawk aspect stuck up so regally from the far too open jacket neck.

Oh, these grandiose, blue-eyed magpie people! If one saw a sled road that went zigzag then one could swear it was the magpie people who had driven up it – the entire West Parish was embroidered with such zigzag roads. They always stood on the right knee in the sled and with the left leg flaunted outside; they struggled and cracked and swung the rein incessantly over the reindeer's back, a jerk here, a jerk there. They hollered and shrieked and yoiked cheering, jerking – all market places resounded and were gaudy with their resplendent colors and boisterous voices. But if one saw a proper sled or a proper knife with them, it was quite obvious that they were bought in the East Parish.

Who then are the magpie people – these towering, blue-eyed people whose heads stretch so roughly up from the jacket neck?

They were once an offshoot of the sailing folks here in the west – an offshoot in so many ways. So new are they still in their second historical separation, to this very day they go astray on these severe plateaus as in an abandonment, have to this very day not been able to fit in this their new existence, – in part maybe also for the reason it has been a backwards development. In their magpie nests on the West Parish's mountains and in the small houses in the west village they go around in their leather clothing until they rot and the hair falls off in large batches. They have somehow not learned to gather clothing around themselves yet – the mountain storms can blow freely into the stiffly resistant jacket. It is as if they were to find themselves in a temporary and indifferent self abandonment. But the indifferent and gradual and purely unknown has become a part of their world.

And then to boot they should land on the highest plateaus up there – the village to the west hasn't seen a single pine in the past hundred years – the residents, those who take care of cows and live in houses, must fetch lumber from districts lying 15-20 miles away. Wherever they turn they are somehow without shelter, and moreover they lack a sense of the intimate – well, then one fires away in one's arrogant and blue-eyed undisturbed free and easyness with brooches and the three- and four-sided, blue and yellow and red pieces of cloth on their stiffly bristling leather clothing.

---

[19] Hairy leggings from the skin of the reindeer's leg, lengthened with a wide piece of red cloth around the ankle; – the leg on the footwear is secured with a two-inch wide artistically woven band, on which the narrow end of this is coiled around the garment, the extension of the bellingen.

The festive, one has at any rate a sense for. One is not for nothing a descendant of the leather clad hordes which Caesar seemed to nourish a certain respect for, and that certainly with good reason. Somehow one also knows how to make an entry of brilliance: riding on red carpets into Constantinople! ... a few golden shoes drop off the hooves of the horses; but Sigurd the Crusader's men don't pay attention to such trifles.

... But as said a serpent had come into the interim with the magpie people. If it was troublesome to get fire to catch in willow scrap in a mountain cabin on the plateau, a magpie man immediately got after tables and benches and lit a magnificent bonfire of them. And if it was too little he got after the walls. The next traveler of a magpie man continued where the first one had begun. And that's how it could go – until one of them sat under open sky and burned a bonfire of the last floor beams in the mountain cabin.

When they somewhat over sixty years ago and a single time in their lives caught a religious rapture, they chased the devil with stakes out of the skeptical minister, stabbed the sheriff to hell and burned the merchant inside.

On reindeer sledges

While all the other young men had each grabbed his own girl for nocturnal cheer in all decency – well, just as the rural youth also in other districts had as a custom in the good, old days –, then Saivo Piera went around the entire night like a hapless, jacket-clad and bedizened spirit looking for Aile.

But Aile was, when you come right down to it, not to be found.

Olle lay on his bed in the small side room; he had it none too good himself either. He got up, – as supervisor he had both the right and duty to inspect. In the large room lay his own, East Parish folks and *Anáraččat* – in the room on the other side of the hall lay the magpie folks. He had quietly arranged it thus, gradually as his Easter guests arrived. He was no fair-haired missionary for whom it was important to be good toward everyone, as our Lord has commanded all of us to be and especially a missionary, – he was as biased and parochial as anyone. And he could also defend this arrangement by its being necessarily hygienic: the magpie folks were as said not busy changing clothes.

The young turtledoves had stuck their beaks into each other's business. Olle saw them in the hall, on the storehouse steps, over by the chapel wall, in the cow barn passage and even way out on the plain. And he saw a man go on skis out over the plain; it was Saivo Piera who was on his way up to Jauna Jauna's camp – oh, Saivo Piera could have saved himself the trouble. Aile was probably not there either.

But when morning arrived Aile was again to be seen; no one knew where she had been during the night; the old women and young girls and the young men couldn't solve the riddle, – first they tried to guess that maybe she had been with Olle; but those who had been in the big room could testify that Olle had been alone all right.

But Saivo Piera was just as persistent; he pretended to be ignorant of the situation. Yes, he even wanted to let it be apparent there was a certain intimacy between her and him, – one could readily believe they had been together during the night, anyway. He also had recourse to the not too bad tactic of capturing Olle's confidence. But he had nevertheless become helplessly confused; he darted around and assisted with all his might, stopped Olle and Aile in season and out; it was a matter of all sorts of things – finally he grabbed the big state church kettle hanging over the fire in the hearth, full of half cooked pieces of meat, and was going to raise it up – of the purest, but also of the most bewildered need of activity Aile in her born days had seen.

"What in the Lord's name are you thinking up?" she shouted and was seriously exasperated.

Saivo sank to his knees, out of fright – he lost his grip on the strap, the kettle thumped against the grate, hit the coal bucket, and hundreds of pieces of meat – all uncooked – poured out over the floor.

The moment's breathless silence was followed by oaths and laughter pouring down. The dogs who resolutely had thrown themselves over this Egyptian surplus of meat, burned themselves in their mouths, were grasped by the neck and heaved and kicked out during an unchristian swearing and reveling.

… And now they were all supposed to go into the chapel, on the first general prayer meeting in the 'Lord's sanctuary' in Helligskogen, and which the Swede had 'sawed lumber for.' Olle had today – to endow the day with a little festive character – sent a man good at tolling the bell to ring the chapel bell. And now he himself stood in jacket and with the book of sermons and hymnal in hand out in the yard to lead the congregation and proceed out to the chapel.

But then old Saivo says:

"Put on your fancy garments, Olle."

Olle was taken aback – fancy garments?

"Yes, put them on, Olle," shouted the others, "we want a proper prayer meeting. Our sexton always has such a garment on when he holds a prayer meeting in the church in the minister's absence."

The appeals became so ardent and determined Olle involuntarily stood there a little lost, and it didn't get any better when he saw Aile standing there giggling. Aile could on the whole be very given to laughter; she had also before made fun of the hapless garment; she had asked him whether he had considered wearing it when he was at a party with them, and she had illustrated how he sat on a provision box and pulled a few hairs off the garment.

Now, Olle pulled himself together, went in and put on the frock coat.

The congregation was so large that the chapel was almost full. Olle stood in the choir door and sang; and when they were finished with the hymn and Olle was going to open the book of sermons, old Saivo who of course was sitting highest up says:

"Go up into the pulpit, Olle."

Olle got confused.

"Yes, go up into the pulpit, you," said another.

"Just go up, you!" chimed in several.

Olle stood there bewildered; he saw a glimpse of Aile who was sitting farthest down by the door. She had her hand in front of her mouth and could surely hardly more than barely not break into a loud laughter. But Saivo Piera who in spite of the accident with the kettle had sought a spot close to her, also wanted to assist her in laughing – he grunted dutifully with a desperately poorly made laughter; but he was paralyzed by a lightning fast glance from Aile and all the others – they began mumbling out loud; yes, a man said even quite loud that Saivo Piera certainly had to have drunk brandy since he came up with something like that in church. But then old Saivo got up at full length and explained loudly and moved and full of conviction:

"No, our Piera does not drink brandy."

"Go up into the pulpit, Olle!" was heard again from many voices.

Olle moved up into the pulpit and recited the day's text and meditation in a strong wrath – it sounded like the entire meditation was full of defamation and words of abuse, and when he was done, he closed the book of sermons so there was a bang 'amen.'

*　　*

*

In the meantime, the most serious and most complicated and prolonged negotiations had been and were still going on between old Saivo and his old woman on the one hand and Jauna Jauna and Gudnel and mother Jauna on the other.

Jauna Jauna was absolutely agreeably disposed; he had always harbored a bewitching admiration for Saivo, this West Parish's gentle miracle who was even the second richest among his people, – otherwise the richest man in the West Parish was a recent immigrant *Hoammá*;[20] he had an *eallu*[21] of over three thousand reindeer and was the owner of a house and storehouse at the church locality. His treasure chest was full of jewels and beakers of gold and silver, old, expensive silk scarves and shawls, and on the walls of the storehouse hung equally old and valuable costumes of scarlet cloth – *Hoammát* are also rich and excellent and handsome people; but because of the old bitter hatred between the two villages this rich person of a *Hoammá* was always regarded as a stranger in the West Parish – and that in spite of his integrity; but it could also lie in the fact that the West Parish people were afraid that someone, even a stranger, might contend for precedence with old Saivo.

Yes, Jauna Jauna was willing enough; he had with his own eyes seen Saivo's *eallu*, and if there is anything that makes an impression on a mountain Sámi then it is the sight of a large and luxuriant reindeer herd. And so otherwise Saivo was also the one he was.

Good heavens, the old one and Gudnel too knew how to evaluate Saivos; but it was so strange when all is said and done: all favorable impressions were lost against the fact Saivos were and are still West Parish folks.

Yes, this was fishing in troubled waters for Gudnel, and even more delightful did it become for her, when also the other young men who had been witnesses to Saivo

---

[20] *Hoammá*, pl. *hoammát* – a man from Kautokeino.

[21] *Eallu* – fortune, most often with an eye to a reindeer herd considered as value.

Piera's equally fruitless as persistent exertions to catch Aile alone, *Gusavuodja*, began to show off – and Aile had again to run the gantlet between affectionate, warm hands as at every door, in every corner, in the hall, at the hearth, everywhere ready to pat her and try to get to perceive a little, cheerful sign from her little, white hand.

Great God, how Gudnel reveled in it! The one who now at the same time could have been down in the village, in the capital, and seen Erki Lemik Issak's son and all the other big dandies down there watch out for and grab Aile in the door and pull her up into the small side room and up onto the large, fine bed – to lie on, of course, – and then out on a driving tour through the village. But it was only Erki Lemik Issak's son who had a fancy sled of the right sort, and he had a young stallion that could trot so the sleigh bells sang like a musical work in heaven.

Oh, this Erki Lemik Issak's son down there – didn't reign over seven parishes just by existing! He was the great *bøyg*[22] everywhere.

But darn it, this couldn't go on for long! Saivos had come on a serious errand; the old one had with her a large bag of party gifts, rings, silver brooches, silk scarves and shawls and a large, wide leather belt tightly studded with small rectangular brooches, *golleboagán*, called the gold belt. The brandy which of course goes with such journeys, because of their faith and for the sake of their renowned good reputation they couldn't attempt to travel with, so much the less as they of course knew the Jauna Jaunas were believers.

But both Jauna Jauna and Saivo had in the old days been whizzes at downing half-pint shots at the counter in the storekeeper's country store down in the village. They had flung one reindeer steak after the other up onto the counter and demanded new, full half-pints of the largest sort.

For a moment old Saivo was daydreaming.

If only they all now, both Saivos and Jauna Jaunas, had been able to sit in overturned sleds here in the yard and drink from beakers. They would have gotten so happy and glad together; they would have held each other around the neck, and they would have yoiked each other's praise, while Piera and Aile lay their heads together. And while the others watched admiringly and enviously that the two chieftains, Saivo and Jauna Jauna, now knotted family ties in this way, then they could have held their child's wedding down there in the big village, with the entire village as guests … Saivo's son and Jauna Jauna's beautiful daughter celebrate their wedding. The church road shines with silk and gold and silver and the reddest red, in sun and snow, while the church bell chimes and the church hill is full of spectators.

… Old Saivo inquired of his son how it was going, and Piera asked his father, how it was going on his part. Then they consulted with the mother, and she wasn't firm; women are so clever at managing in passing when it's a matter of such opportunities. She advised Piera to yield on Hoammá Čuonja,[23] and Piera grabbed at this last resort if not exactly with greed, then in any case with a certain relief.

---

[22] Obstacle that can be felt, cf. Ibsen's "Peer Gynt."

[23] *Čuonjá* – goose, nickname in a good sense.

But from now on Jauna Jauna thought something bad and gloomy had come over old Saivo's face.

There wasn't a 'no' in Hoammá Čuonja's mouth, and Saivos let it be understood too it actually was her they had originally thought about.

*   *
*

Already the same evening people got to work.

Hoammá Čuonja's parents had together with Saivo and mother Saivo been seated highest up in the large room at the request of the best man, – mother Saivo had the important belt in her lap that is a part of such an occasion. The room and the hall and the small side room were chock-full of people.

The lamp over the long table was lit, and Olle had expended several candles so it would look really festive. Outside it was dark, and Hoammá Čuonja had presumably hidden herself in the storehouse or the cow barn or wherever it might be – it was somehow important to be a little hard to get an answer out of –, and now Saivo Piera went out there and looked for her.

The best man hauls a bottle and a beaker up from his jacket chest – well, for old Saivo had forgotten about himself; it had happened during the day's dark assaults; so fatefully serious had the defeat been.

But now everyone looks toward the door; Saivo Piera comes in tugging the modest and plump Hoammá Čuonja. He is noisily in high spirits, and elegantly and confidently he places her and himself on the bench highest up. The best man pours around; he also finds some among the spectators who must be honored with a dram.

Then he begins to speak. He intends now, he says, on behalf of Saivo Piera, whose snowwhite reindeer flies over the snowy plateau like the ptarmigan flies on its wings – the only son of Saivo, this godfearing man whom everyone, all people, also ministers and bailiffs and bishops and administrative officers honor as first in the West Parish, – yes, on behalf of Saivo Piera he intends now to ask Hoammá Čuonja's parents for consent that the two, the most beautiful goose and the most honorable young man on the mountain, may unite by the fireside of love and happiness in their own tent.

"Yes," said Hoammá Čuonja's old, unassuming father, "when it is now Saivo's son who asks for our daughter's hand, then both mother and I say yes to that," – and the old one turned toward Čuonja and said somehow more intimate: "Well, what do you say yourself, Magga?"

The bashful and stunning Magga-Čuonja fidgeted with her eyes and twisted her mouth back and forth; of course, there was not a no in her mouth, but yes was such a difficult word; her mother had to come to her assistance, she said, that Magga would.

And while mother Saivo unties the knot on the bundle and begins to lay the celebration gifts on Čuonja's lap – shawls, silk scarves, rings, brooches and the large

65

'gold belt' – *golleboagán*, the best man goes around and pours another round from the beaker bowl. The atmosphere was already unlimited – for there had been more bottles here than anything else – the West Parish folks' magnificent hawk aspect stretched more than ever up from the jacket collar.

"Saivo Piera!" they shout from all directions. "Old Saivo, the West Parish's pride and joy!"

Also *Hoammát* and the East Parish people and *Anáraččat* and the Swedish knit caps are swept along "Saivo Piera! Old Saivo! Mother Saivo! Hoammá Čuonja!" – and the tightly packed masses of jackets in the overheated room are alive and roar like a choppy sea in a bay; the faces flush feverishly; they embrace each other and yoik at the top of their voices: "Saivo lulila, Saivo Piera, Hoammá Čuonja lali lali lulila."

"Never has there lived such a man on the mountain than old Saivo! But now old Saivo too jumps up; he is *gárremiin*.[24] On the sober it made a downright appalling impression to see all the bad, raw and confounded that actually welled out of his countenance – God help them, beware this Saivo!

"I'm rich!" he shrieked.

"The richest in the entire West Parish," shouted his enthusiastic compatriots.

"I'm the richest of all Sámi; I'm just as rich as some merchants in the towns. H. Savings bank is in my pocket," – and foam poured out of his mouth when he cleared the way over to Jauna Jauna:

"I've never stolen so much as a miserable *čearpmat*.[25] I don't know whether you can say the same about yourself, Jauna Jauna."

The peaceful Jauna Jauna who had always been a genuine admirer of Saivo had however become so dismayed at seeing this frightful transformation of Saivo that he wasn't able to reply. Had it even been Piera or anyone else – but Saivo, this old gentleman and the people's saint, him *gárremiin*! And then behave like the worst of the magpie people …

It was as if Jauna Jauna should have been witness to an old Christian beginning to drink brandy and swear on his deathbed.

"I am not only a believer; I am the one who believes most of all," shrieked the big, old Saivo, waved his arms and looked terribly fierce. But then there were some who began laughing, and that laughter was inevitably contagious; there was no demand for it.

… But what happened to Saivo Piera? His otherwise so high-born head began to hang down – was he drunk? – it didn't look like that either. His look seems to grope toward the door; he breathes heavily every so often – Hoammá Čuonja doesn't seem to exist for him any more, and heaven have mercy; he bursts into tears … yes, for Aile stood down there by the door, and he seemed to notice there lay a shadow of remorse over her little delightful face … and she was more beautiful than ever.

---

[24] Intoxicated.
[25] *Čearpmat* – one year old reindeer calf.

Saivo Piera couldn't take any more; he got up loudly sobbing and hurried out; it was as if he was hurrying out of a burning house.

Mother Saivo and the best man after; they found him behind the barn where he stood leaning against the wall and acting like a mortally wounded animal.

"What is it? What is this supposed to mean?" his mother asks. Piera sobbed and stammered out something about not being able to. Not in any way. They had to go in and say that he couldn't.

Now, there was nothing else to do. The best man shuffled in and said something was terribly wrong with Piera, that he at the moment was unable … But just as the best man was on the point of displaying all his eloquence and was right in his element of smoothing things over, Hoammá Čuonja's mother got up in all her finery – wild and exasperated – for which she could not be blamed – and said:

"Well, Saivo Piera can just get lost!"

And now there arose a Babylonian confusion; everyone's hand was turned against everyone.

And on top of all this the magpie people suddenly discovered Olle had deliberately separated them from the others and placed them in the room on the other side of the passage. In a body and shouting and swearing they flew after their provision bags and jackets and coffee pots and took possession of the big room – in a moment this room was transformed into a little Noah's ark in rebellion.

"And if it gets too cramped in here then we'll – the devil toss me – soon make it roomier," shouted a grandiose hawk face of a West Parisher.

That wasn't all. It dawned more sharply and greater on them.

It was Olle who had reduced Saivo Piera's happiness to rubble. He who was also to blame for Bittoš Hansa's death – hadn't he simply killed Bittoš Hansa during the fight. And how had he not read the Scripture in the chapel today? And he walks around here and plays the fine gentlemen and keeps the small side room to himself?

He's the one we are going to have as host and holder of prayer meetings here in Helligskogen. What are they doing with him here? And who the hell had gotten him up here?

It had first been the intention to get a farmer Sámi from the East Parish up here as host, the excellent and beloved Ommuk who had a family, was a serious and devout man, had cows and sheep and could have lived like a well-off farmer up here.

"Go after water then, Olle! And wood too! And fire in the hearth, damn it!"

But during the hullaballoo one of Olle's protegés, a *Hoammá*, who went by the nickname *Bihcebásloddi*[26] – his mouth was crooked to the left, his owl nose to the right – he comes pulling a sled, lifts it up and holds it up to the light:

"See, here you see a sled, folks. One can see the sky and the forest through this remarkable sled. And one can sit in it; one can hide under it and imagine a dan-

---

[26] Crossbill, a tiny little bird.

gerous bear, that there is just a little pile of debarked sticks of wood … Who was responsible for this sled?"

Well, for this *Hoammá* and *Bihcebásloddi* would somehow make fun of the West Parish folks; he was taken by the neck and tossed out and got the sled on his rear to boot. But Bihcebásloddi, who didn't seem to bother a bit more or less, went out and used his jaw against these *báhkinat*,[27] who couldn't leave people alone. And in again, yelled out he wouldn't be in the same room as the magpie people, and gave the signal for a quick and joyous fight between the magpie people on the one side and *Hoammát* and East Parish people and *Anáraččat* and the Swedish knit caps on the other side. Which was sorely welcome for Olle who now got clear lines and a loyal majority.

But loudest and most unpleasant of all fumed old Saivo; he had most literally gone out of his mind, broke cups and bottles, knocked out a couple windows in Olle's place and shook everyone off who tried to make him listen to reason.

"I am not only devout; I am the one who believes most of all! I've been sent by God; I have the largest herd on the entire earth," and Saivo's look flashed where he stood with his fists planted on either side, this, the blue-eyed magpie folks' top figure and holy miracle, he who actually hadn't stolen so much as a tattered *čearpmat* in his life, and who actually hadn't tasted a single drop of brandy in way over a generation.

"I will be God's king over all Sámi, over the East Parish folks, over *Anáraččat*, over the Swedish and Russian and also over many *dáččat*."[28]

Finally they had to resort to the way out of overpowering him and tying him up. He continued to rage far into the night when he finally grew weak and fell asleep.

---

[27] *Báhkinat* (pl.) – heathens, from Lat. Paganus, originally dweller in the province.
[28] *Dáččat* – alternative form of *dárru* (Norwegian language).

On vehicles drawn by reindeer

But in the morning old Saivo had disappeared. Nor did he have anything else to do.

Piera and mother Saivo had thought it right to refrain from fleeing; it can sometimes be an advantage to stand face to face with the ruins, and when these didn't seem worse to them than one could surely stand the sight of them, why then give oneself the last coup de grace which a flight as a rule is and in this case also absolutely would have been.

And the people can often be better than their reputation; that Piera and mother Saivo also had experienced – likewise the other West Parish folks who had no reason either to be arrogant after the evening's escapades.

And that they could mostly thank Olle for. He was the first one up today, lit a fire in both rooms and greeted the people friendly and cheerfully elated, as they awakened. He joked and laughed off the whole thing and spoke about good weather and other things that could call attention to other good earthly things than such as had happened yesterday evening. And he spoke alone with those he knew well among the others that they all had to make an effort to forget about the whole thing and live united as is fitting for good Christians.

And the Good Friday prayer meeting in the chapel turned into a real experience for all of them – of course, Olle could do it once he settled into the old grooves, and never had they heard anyone sing hymns so beautifully and uplifting as Olle.

Yes, here reigned the pure idyl this day; everyone was in such a good mood and friendly toward each other, – real fun to be in Helligskogen now.

… It occurred to Olle that the fire room in the cow barn could be used as a room for hot steam baths. And no sooner said than done. He got someone to dig up stones under the snow down by the river and drive them up. And he piled them up into a thick wall around the large barn kettle which was filled with water to the rim. He lit a fire underneath, and when the whole stone wall had been heated up, he poured water over it, and it turned into vigorous steam.

One of the first things a Kven takes care of when as a new settler he settles down somewhere in the wilderness to clear and build, is to set up a sauna, but no more artificial than Olle's.

So the Sámi were familiar with the sauna, and some of them from Sweden and Finland had perhaps also themselves been in a sauna sometime in their life.

… Well, some of the youth were so heedless they wanted to take the opportunity.

And Aile was going to wash clothes for Olle, and for that reason a fire place was also made out in the yard. And when Aile was done with Olle's clothing, there were some who thought it might be fun to wash a kerchief or such.

It all ended up as a single purification fest all of Easter. Those who to begin with just laughed at it, or at the most wanted to be content with a face wash, were swept along or simply forcefully carried into the sauna. For maybe there was something to it, what Olle said, – it was of no use to believe in the holy trinity, when people didn't follow the first of all commandments: be pure! Uncleanliness was the devil's device and best weapon; when everything else failed for him, then he drew the veil of uncleanliness between the people and the savior's pure stature. Yes, wasn't it uncleanliness itself which all of life carried on an eternal struggle with? Life came into existence at that moment when there arose a dividing line between the pure and impure. Lightning and thunder, the flood and death and snow and cold and sun – they carried on all of God's great war against uncleanliness. And our Lord even had to have recourse to pestilence and the great war when he thought that a common washing with soap wouldn't be of benefit.

Right now was it. There was no other difference between good and evil than that which lay between cleanliness and uncleanliness.

And from Good Friday afternoon and all the way to the fifth and sixth Easter day clothes were hanging out to dry in Helligskogen – the ravens made big detours when early in the morning they flew over the valley and in the evening turned back again. There wasn't a suspicious garment that wasn't boiled and washed. And all leather clothing was pounded in the snow. People changed and changed. Even the last obstinate old fellows and old women had had to give in.

And now people went and strutted in the washed rooms and out in the yard in the loveliest Easter sun; they actually were reflected in each other's transfigured countenance and were sincerely enraptured. To be sure, it felt somewhat cold and unfamiliar when one didn't have the old, tight skin on themselves any more, and they were compelled to go in bare leather clothing, while the homespun clothes were hung out to dry, and some were coughing too; but what difference did that make when one for once in one's life one could feel absolutely clean.

Oh, how the magpie people were handsome, now in the literal sense they had shed their skin. All the other things were mere trifles when it came right down to it.

But the spring air was sharp, and the unfamiliar attire contributed to people beginning to cough ominously much; there was no rest at night because of the coughing. And already the second Easter day no fewer than sixteen people had come down with a virulent pneumonia. They died one after the other; they were essentially old women and men, but also a few younger ones died – merciful God! They died like flies right in front of the dismayed Olle's eyes. Now he was going to witness Hellig-skogen sending bodies to all four corners of the world – northward and up the two valleys above – and westward and … no, it was just as well to bury the eleven dead here in Helligskogen. It didn't make any difference if the bodies lay in unhallowed earth for a while. The minister would of course come up here anyway next winter, and then he could consecrate the graveyard.

Olle measured a bit around the chapel and said this will be the graveyard. They dug the graves, and Olle suggested the departed should be buried in their respective driving sleds. But a couple of the bereaved thought it was probably hard to sacrifice a driving sled; an ordinary load sled would suffice if one put a couple extra boards over it. And there were a few boards left from last year when the carpenters had been here "för at såga timmer til Herrens helgedom."[29]

But Saivo Piera, whose mother was also dead, said she should be burried in her own driving sled, and when the graveyard was consecrated he would pay for a beautiful cross on her grave.

Hoammá Čuonja's mother too had succumbed to pneumonia, and she was also buried in her own sled.

Only the Finnish *Anáraččat* took their dead with them – they had ninety miles to drive to the Enare church grounds.

It would turn out well that it snowed on those days the burials took place. It was as if God himself wanted to make amends a little for the deficient and lay a gleam of commemorative service over such serious religious ceremonies as these … The people have lived; but now they are dead and will be lowered into the earth. They will never again see their loved ones on this earth. Nor will they ever again get to see the herd and the forest; they will never again get to see the sun shine over the plateaus. They are dead – yes, they are dead, and no one has beheld this which many have dimly perceived – no, for the day we were able to behold it we would die.

Here at the grave we stop in your name, you inscrutable one.

Hallowed be thy name.

---

[29] To saw lumber for the Lord's sanctuary.

On the very large number and size of trees
in the northern countries

And now they were all gone. Only the Jauna Jaunas up there on the mountainside were left. But on an early morning in two weeks they too would tackle their big, long migration up to one of the peninsulas to the north where every year they usually had their summer quarters. Every spring all mountain Sámi from the interior and down to the coastal districts head down to the Norwegian coast farther south. It is just the Finnish who don't have access to the sea, – in the summer they usually move closer to the large Lake Enare with its hundreds of islands.

If Olle were to remain here then he wouldn't get to see a living soul until well into the autumn, sometime in October at the earliest.

And if Olle were able to remain here at all, then he had to – well, frankly speaking, then he had to have a wife. That side of the matter he had entrusted to fate when he came up here – or more correctly: he had shut his eyes toward that sort of thing as to so much else; he had just taken a chance; after all that was even his way of going through life – Helligskogen was certainly a good place to settle down at, so it was okay – good God, it was just a matter of … well, good God, what was it a matter of? At a confusing moment a person must be allowed to think it's a matter of the one thing.

Olle then had to be allowed to think it was possible to atone for a misdeed such as his by annihilating himself. And after the inquiry that night he had at such small moments of reckoning with himself somehow only the one misdeed on his conscience. Also now, when he had somehow come out of his first dismay at the sad conclusion to the Easter celebration, that night came over him and delivered him to a distance from all the rest. What did it concern him that a Bittoš Hansa drank himself to death on brandy slush – was it something to feel troubled about that a dozen reindeer Sámi couldn't tolerate washing?

To begin with it was unpleasant enough to think about having the dead in unhallowed ground as neighbors – and in such a situation we are governed of course by what has taken root in us, while we were children – and he had thought about getting Jauna Jauna to be here during the nights – until he got used to the company of the dead people. But he had again become obsessed with 'Cheerful Tenacity' –

again and again he returned to the chapel to walk around the sandy mounds the dead lay under; it was sort of as if he found a kind of solace in this revolt against himself. Yes, during the night while he still lay awake he fought a tickling desire to tear open the window and shout into the night and over to those beneath the sand mounds at the chapel: "You are surely mistaken; you don't live here!" But he checked himself and said seriously and aloud to himself: "Beware, Olle! Beware, what is said will come true. No, that must not happen, my God, that must not happen!"

... Aile had regretted she hadn't traveled down to the village at Easter, and heaven knows whether she also hadn't regretted much else. The day after Saivo Piera's tragic flight from Hoammá Čuonja she had somehow begun to see him with other eyes – oh, Olle had seen it so well, and he understood it so sincerely well ... do what Saivo Piera had done, – see, only a person does that who loves, greatly and seriously and fatefully, and Aile in spite of everything couldn't help it that it made a deep impression on her – apart from the fact that it tickled her vanity.

And what had Olle himself done? Out of pure fear of a possible opposition he had demonstrated with his indifference even when they had been alone in the small side room. And yet – oh, she had seen it so well and had become ashamed – nevertheless, his eyes drooped at her young body, when she went bustling around in only the loose, light costume that draped two young, proud breasts into an absolutely bewitching sight ... and his eyes had sought relief in her pure countenance and in her golden hair which shone brightly and gushed out of the little cap with ear ends for tying under the chin, but which Aile never tied.

'Cheerful Tenacity' had at times wavered badly enough. Olle had to grant that. Life is strong and victorious.

... One morning Jauna Jauna comes down and says the herder who had left with Bittoš Hansa's body, had still not returned home, and he thought this was beginning to look rather suspicious. The herder had now been away for three weeks, – to be sure, one didn't travel according to a timetable in these districts, but nevertheless. Olle thought the herder maybe had wanted to kill two birds with one stone and started to celebrate Easter in the West Parish.

Well, maybe. And then it was time to hit the coffee and a few pipes of tobacco at the long table in the large room.

They spoke first a while about old Saivo, and Jauna Jauna who had been seriously dismayed by what had happened with the old wonder of an honorable man; he said now quite coldblooded it would have been better had old Saivo died instead of his wife.

"Young people," he said, "they can endure falling into sin; they can fall deep; but they can recover. And it is sort of not so shocking when a young person goes wrong than when it happens with an old person. Youth sins often more from inexperience and dissolution than from cold calculation. Now, in a way I can probably excuse old Saivo; it was a difficult blow for a man of his stature, and then of course the fact that in this way it should dawn on him he was no more than a West Parish person when it came right down to it. Yes, it was as if I hadn't thought about it myself either. We had always looked up to Saivos. But when it was seriously discussed that our Aile should become Saivo Piera's wife, – see, then it sort of dawned on us – Saivos were of course West Parish people; respectable and devout for sure; but they were West Parish folks. And when this happened with old Saivo, then we were all, both my wife and Gudnel and our son-in-law, in agreement it was good nothing came of it."

... No, old Saivo was nevertheless a West Parisher when it came down to it. But as said – to see an old man who has even been a devout honorable man all his days, to see him fall into sin is an unpleasant sight ... he gave himself away late; but he gave himself away badly. For that man it will be difficult to recover, and I cannot say other than I fear he will become a dangerous enemy of mine ... if God shouldn't get the upper hand on the evil in him. And I will also say to you, Olle: be careful of Saivos. They probably think our daughter is in love with you. Well, let her worry about that, and if you like her, please. But otherwise there's no hurry. You two must think about it first.

That was forthright information, Olle thought, and it came so suddenly he at the moment had nothing else to say but "that is so."

*　　*
*

While Olle the same evening is sitting by the hearth and planing a couple of sled runners, he hears someone driving stop outside – it occurred to him it couldn't be Jauna Jauna or any of the others from the mountainside up there; he quite simply got a shock. He dreads going out, just sits there and listens with a pounding heart. Then he hears the person fumble for the doorknob.

The door opens up, and in walks the herder who went away with Bittoš Hansa's mortal remains. He looks like a pure ghost, says nothing, not even good evening. Olle gets up, and the two stand there like two speechless souls in purgatory and gape at each other with uneasy glances. Finally, Olle collects himself and says:

"Has something happened, Nilas?"

"Yes, something has happened to me – God have mercy on me!"

But there was nothing to get out of him for the time being. Olle hung the kettle and coffeepot up, and when Nilas had eaten and drunk coffee and gotten his pipe lit, he began to liven up a little.

Things had gone for him in the following way: the first day everything went well. Later in the evening he reached a mountain lake which lay down in a hollow, and he decided to drive over it too before he set up night quarters.

He had already gotten far onto the ice when it occurs to him it's *Jápmu-jávri;*[30] he is driving over. He looks back, and he thinks the reindeer pulling the corpse sled has gotten so oddly fidgety; it lifts its back legs up under its belly; yes, it's as if it wanted to howl. Nevertheless, he didn't mind it that much to begin with. But when

---

[30] *Jápmu-jávri* – Deadman's Lake.

he again looks back, he thinks that the braking reindeer too has begun to behave in the same way. Wolves or other beasts it couldn't be – otherwise things would have been different.

And instead of it growing darker it begins to get so oddly light around; it had nothing to do with the moon or northern lights, no, it was a light that had risen up from the ice and snow itself. He could see far into the birch scrubs on the beachs, and there it swarmed with ptarmigans.

Then it was as if a heavy crash went through the ice on the lake; it gurgled along the banks; there were steps under the sled he himself was sitting in – finally, it was as if the ice wept … and everything was shrouded in darkness again, and it became still, yes, good heavens how it became still!

Nilas burst into tears while he sat here at the hearth and told Olle this.

Now, from that moment he couldn't remember what had happened afterwards that evening – well, one thing or other he probably thought he remembered, but didn't know whether it had been dream or reality.

He didn't get a grip on himself until towards morning, – then he was driving down from another plateau, – and he discovered both the body and the sled were gone; but the reindeer he had behind him.

But he continued to drive on. He thought though he must have taken a breather during the night; for the reindeer seemed to be fresh and in fine fettle.

Then he came across a reindeer camp down in a little valley on the plateau. Here he told what errand he was on and what had happened to him on Deadman's Lake. But he hadn't gotten anyone to come along to try to find the corpse, and alone he couldn't manage to do it. And then he had been lying in that reindeer camp all that time. Finally, he found a remedy; he could take a detour to avoid Deadman's Lake. It had been slow going; for he had had no cleared sled road to stay on.

"Well, you see," he says. "Deadman's Lake takes its own. A person who dies the way Bittoš Hansa did, will not get across Deadman's Lake. It is not immaterial how we humans withdraw from life, for we somehow have two souls, one that will stand forth before God and one that remains. The one must give an accounting before God, the other for the people here on earth. But we shouldn't judge Bittoš Hansa according to what happened to him the last day he lived. God's spirit also follows the soul gone astray, and much probably happens on death's threshold which we humans don't know about."

Yes, Nilas had become wise on this journey, and he was an intelligent man otherwise too. He asked Olle to read out loud the ritual for the dead and sing a couple of hymns. Yes, Olle really wanted to do that; it was a solace too for himself to get to do it. And Nilas sat with folded hands and listened while the tears dampened his cheeks and beard.

On the variety of trees

Jauna Jauna didn't think it was worth the trouble so long afterwards to try to find Bittoš Hansa's mortal remains. But Nilas nevertheless was allowed to go with Olle. They looked everywhere around Deadman's Lake, unfortunately in vain. But Olle had in any case done his part, and that was always a comfort.

There was something that deeply concerned Jauna Jauna recently. The mountain Sámi had by all means to leave the interior in May and not appear there again until in September. Could such a law be proper? It wasn't like that in the old days.

No, no, Olle thought. But the law was in the best interests of the mountain Sámi. Reindeer moss which grows so extremely slowly has to be conserved in here; it must be protected part of the year. And of course the Sámi had also in the old days, long before the statutory provision came, been in the habit of migrating northward during the summer, preferably up to the districts around the Gaisa glaciers on the big, long peninsula to the north. There the reindeer could be free of the mosquito nuisance, drink a little sea water and breathe in the ocean fresh air.

Yes, that was probably so. But Jauna Jauna wanted at any rate to have it established that it couldn't be regarded as a sin against God if a mountain Sámi thinks it fit to spend the summer here in the interior; "if his reindeer didn't cause damage to the Sámi farmers' outlying fields and their moss-covered mountain plateaus around the village."

"Sin against God, it could of course be depending on how you take it. But you'll be fined, maybe punished, if it is discovered."

Well, that was that … But he knew someone who had done it a few years ago.

Really. Well, Olle had also in the old days known about someone who had done the same thing.

… Jauna Jauna stayed away a couple days. But when he again appeared down at Olle's, he had sort of become so odd and strange, so taciturn. He fumbled from one thing to another. Only when he had gotten some cups of coffee in him and lit his pipe did he again begin to liven up. And then he suddenly and quite definitely said:

"It's too bad."

"What?"

"Well, you know. We are going to obey the authorities. It's ordained by God."

On salmon-fishing

Jauna Jauna is busy leaving to set to work on the migration up to the summer quarters between the Gaisa glaciers to the north.

It will take four to five weeks for them to get there – it's a good twenty-five *beanagullan*[31] up there.

There is more than just sunshine and mild weather today. The forest and the air are full of a stifling fragrance, and the snow masses glitter feverishly.

Olle is sitting on a sled outside Jauna Jauna's tent up here on the mountainside and watching, while Aile and the others are busy packing pots and containers and kettles and jackets and blankets and much else down in the baggage sleds – there is nevertheless unbelievably much a mountain Sámi can have in the way of kitchen utensils when it comes down to it.

Gudnel's and Little-Andi's tent has already been taken down, and the brown singed tent covers with the tent poles on top are wrapped and secured in a couple of the largest baggage sleds.

The dogs were beside themselves – now there was going to be a festive trip over the plateaus, with the whole herd in front. And Gudnel's and Little-Andi's three small kids could never finish trying in which order they were going to sit in the big 'family sled' the three were going to have jointly. One wanted to sit this way, another that way.

Jauna Jauna was an equally unostentatious as splendid man; he presented Olle with a fine driving reindeer – "then you won't have to be a draft animal yourself."

"But poor you, Olle, who is going to be alone here in Helligskogen," Gudnel says. "I don't know any other way out than for Aile to stay here with you."

"I take you at your word, Gudnel," Olle joked.

"No, that will not be," says mother Jauna seriously and determined. "What would people say about Aile then? And what would one say if the supervisor and prayer leader in Helligskogen has a young girl with him alone."

---

[31] *Beanagullan* – the farthest distance within which a dog's bark can be heard, about six miles. *Beana* – dog. *Gullan*, from *gullát* – to begin to hear.

"A bachelor surely must be allowed to have a housekeeper," – of course, it is Gudnel who says this, "And Aile can sleep in the room on the north side of the hall – and lock the door by all means if it's going to be so precise."

They laughed all of them, except Aile; that was enough of the joke too, she thought.

But Olle sat here in a worse dilemma than anyone suspected. He had neglected himself – neglected himself to the extent he was completely at sea. And now it was too late to make up for lost time … Here was Aile packing; she was wearing only a jacket in all the bustle and in this penetrating spring warmth, and everytime she straightened up, her young, insolent breasts lifted her jacket so high up that it hardly reached down to her knees.

Saivo Piera in any case she wouldn't meet until far into the fall; for the West Parish people had their summer quarters on another peninsula to the north, farther west. And make a detour down to the east village on the way, down to Erki Lemik Issak's son's village, there was not time for that now so late in the spring.

But Olle's mind didn't allow itself to be put off by that sort. He had neglected himself. She had often been alone down at his place … A bishop ought to be inviolable and the like – … Bittoš Hansa was dead – and how many others were dead? – and otherwise? … – everything he had carried out here in Helligskogen had been so harebrained even 'cheerful tenacity' wouldn't have been able to bring about much more of that sort. Maybe it partly stemmed from his – unbeknownst to himself – still not having gotten any secure faith that Helligskogen really was going to be his home. That sort of thing undermines.

… Aile goes into the empty tent to loosen the ropes around the tent poles. Olle walks in to help her. There's a knot Aile in a way can't untie. Olle wants to try; he reaches over her with her head between his arms. Then the feminine fragrance causes his senses to catch on fire; she notices it and becomes dizzy, – a kiss that will not slacken, and they sink down onto the birch twig bed …

… Afterwards they took the tent down, and they were happy, as if they had won more than the great lottery, – they had managed to escape from a threatening darkness and into a bright and secure reality.

… The reindeer were hitched to the driving and cargo sleds, and the family string, Jauna Jauna, mother Jauna, Aile, Gudnel and Little-Andi and their three kids started off up over the wooded slopes. Olle was going to accompany them a ways up on the plateau; he drove with the reindeer he had gotten as a present from Jauna Jauna. And the forest was sparse enough up here that now and then he could drive alongside Aile. Yes, for they sort of acknowledged it now, and the others were silent happily acquiesing.

Then they ran into the herd which the herders, the two reaŋggat,[32] had gathered up there where the pine forest ends. It was a herd of about two thousand reindeer of which six hundred were Gudnel's and Little-Andi's.

---

[32] Reaŋggat, pl. of reaŋga – hired hand, hired boy.

They stopped here to take leave of Olle.

"But now you could just as well stay here until the fall," Olle says to Jauna Jauna. "That couldn't make any difference for a single time. And I will of course keep quiet. about it."

"Oh no," Jauna Jauna said, "that's not possible." After all, Olle said it also mostly to be good to Aile.

"But you can of course come with us," Gudnel says. "It's hard to know what Aile might think up when you are not along to take care of her."

See, it was of course a pleasant mixture of jest and seriousness. And Olle saw willingly that there was very much jest in the seriousness this time. The helping hand he had given Aile in the tent before it was taken down had quite certainly turned into a milestone in his life here in Helligskogen, and the seriousness with him had awakened; but the whole thing somehow hadn't had time to mature yet in these few hours.

Yes, what really had been the longer-term plan for him when he headed up here to Helligskogen – directly over the western mountains and not up the valley and past the east village down there? – if one were at all going to talk about long-term plans for a man who had gotten going the way Olle had, and who mostly was given to going with the flow. But of course he was not entirely without plans.

When the mountain Sámi had left the districts around here, he would continue staying here well into the summer making small preparations, for one thing, be busy with clearing when the deep frost had melted. Then after 'the spring work' he would go down to the east village to pick up a cow – one cow was enough to begin with – a riverboat, a wife, fishing net and various other things. The cow the wife could walk with, and then he could get a man to help him pole the boat and the goods up the river.

But the core of the plan was of course this with the wife, and this he had of course already in a way brought to light. … But still – purely instinctively he was opposed to being pressed by Gudnel to say a single binding word. He didn't conceal that he loved Aile. What happened in the tent had kindled in him a serious attachment for her and a new and footloose view of the future. But it had also made him strong and lucid … this would have to take care of itself.

… Then the herders gave the dogs a signal, and so cursed had these been at reveling in this signal the first baying was stuck in the throat, they sort of had to swallow it first; but then a whining of dogs without equal was raised, and ragged little things began to sweep the huge herd upward, up toward the bare, level plateau which with a gradual ascent cut into the skyline to the north.

One of the herders went on skis in front and led a couple of bell reindeer after himself.

The string of sleds followed after; the dogs continued to bay at the top of their lungs – in spite of the people's scolding and indignant lectures – it was also now too much to ask that they should be able to shut up during such a departure and in such devilish weather.

Olle stood down here at the timberline and watched. The herd flowed in a large width up over the snowy plateau; it receded and receded, and the dog baying and the human voices receded. But one could still hear the distant splashing of the little pelting rain on the reindeer's toe joints, and the herd undulated and gleamed and was alive as a distant vision of a choppy sea. Aile sat backwards in the sled and waved. Poor little, fair Aile – what is it she wanted to have said? – that he didn't have to travel down to the village this summer. She had in these couple hours glowed from a new joy, from a new sincerity – everything had gotten so big and new.

The little blue silk kerchief on her head was the last thing he saw between the snow rim to the north.

… On the broad path the herd had tramped up in the snow lay behind shed antlers here and there and a few blood spots – at this time of the year the reindeer shed their antlers, and a few animals in Jauna Jauna's herd had already begun to get new antlers, just cartilage projections to begin with and covered with hairy hide for protection during the growth.

And in fourteen days the female reindeer would begin to calve, and then the Jauna Jaunas would have to take a few days rest, separate the bulls and otherwise run around as if possessed. It happens the female reindeer tramples to death its own offspring or leaves it in the lurch, and one has to be careful that she smells it, so she can be convinced this creature is her universal duty to take care of.

That reindeer calf is going to be Olle's, says Aile to herself; but she won't say it to others – well, maybe she can say it to Gudnel all the same.

And that one there is my calf – and that is mine – and that mine, shout the kids and run around as if possessed.

… Then it's time to depart again. … It has turned into summer in the mountains too. The Jauna Jaunas have their summer tents of canvas by a little mountain lake with green grass and rushes around, and on the hills around are crowberries and heather. On the calm, sunlit nights they sit by the fire outside the tent. The sun's reflection streams through the heather on the heights and through the green grass and rushes around the shiny calm lake, and it streams over the snow-white and icy green glacier far away and high up. The Jauna Jaunas have met people and reindeer herds from other districts and heard news from the east village and from the towns and the wider world. And they themselves could tell news from Helligskogen, where they had lived in the lap of luxury at Easter. There had come *Anáraččat* from Finland and many reindeer Sámi from Sweden. There were also many West Parish folks and *Hoammát*. But quite a few people died at Helligskogen at Easter because they had been in the sauna. They were buried in unconsecrated ground. And Olle's driver had died in a tragic way – even the body had disappeared so to speak by itself, while the herder was driving over Deadman's Lake. And the renowned Saivo in the West Parish had in Helligskogen been possessed by the evil one, because Aile wouldn't have his son; he swore maliciously and drank brandy, the old, pious man, and he would certainly never again appear before people but live like a fallen old man in lonely regions and think about bad deeds.

Yes, much stands in new and illuminated light for the Jauna Jaunas too, now, while they are sitting by the fire and in the sun's reflection outside the summer tents and discussing what has happened to them. The birch bark rings on the fishing net in the lake begin to duck here and little waves spread out on both sides of the shining calm water, – the trout has taken its first morning round in the deep water. A golden plover rises up from a gray flat stone in the heather up on a ridge, sings with its long, curved and chattering beak a trembling, sad, mountain plateau tone and sinks slowly with wary, dispirited wing beats down onto another gray flat stone.

One early morning Jauna Jauna and Little-Andi and Aile take off with a few pack reindeer to buy coffee and sugar and flour and decorative material and such at the merchant down by the fjord. Later in the afternoon they reach the high mountain slope that opens up to the sea, – the large, powerful and ever alien blue ocean. They see ships, some with smoke and others with sails, and the waves boom up toward the sky, and it is as if they fall asleep in the air.

And then they climb down. In the deciduous forest Aile stops at a little brook and washes her face and hands, takes the blue silk kerchief on her head, and takes off her *gápmat*[33] to shake up the sedge grass and tie the red decorated bands properly around the uppers of the boots.

Everyone stands looking at Aile in the country store and out in the yard; but even the Norwegian dandies can't get around to making bold approaches to her. Well, they should just try! Aile has, to be sure, greater respect for herself than that – she who is going to be mistress of the house at Helligskogen, she who is going to be Olle's little wife.

… And Olle smiled where he was standing at the timberline and thinking about her and the others who had just disappeared between the sky and the snow line to the north.

---

[33] *Gáma (Norw. komag, pl. komager) – soft, reindeer hide boots.*

How the Lapps hunt

I t's the end of June. And Olle is still here in Helligskogen.

Well, one could almost have been tempted to say it was a heroic act of him to stay here alone. And what is more: he took to foot when the first feelings of loneliness began to rummage around in him, so it boomed in his diaphragm, and let him feel the torments of seasickness. He managed by himself and got better sooner than expected. A glorious morning joy flowed through his blood vessels, and he thanked God for his still being at Helligskogen.

But this time he had probably also been led more by imprudence than by a maturely calculated plan. After all, it was his way of being prepared in this world: let 'er rip. After all, it had gone well, – this sort of thing had happened to him before too; but it had happened more often that things had gone to hell. But hell has, as everyone knows, ways out – for those who are still able to look around after an exit.

After all, he could thank his reindeer for his having dared to let 'er rip. If it didn't work, – well, then one drove off.

All spring he hasn't fired a single shot. There were no other quixotic reasons that had kept him from it other than he didn't want to frighten the birds and animals away from Helligskogen. He needed their company. Jauna Jauna had wanted to present him with a dog; but Olle didn't want a dog. If he wanted fresh meat, he set up a couple of catch fences in some willow bushes above the plain where it swarmed with spring and love mad ptarmigans, but he always removed the snares when he had gotten enough, and three to four ptarmigans were always enough. Up on the mountainside he had a couple hunting huts for wood grouse and had gotten a male black grouse. But when mating time began, he removed the snares there too.

In the morning hours whole droves of hares could be grazing on the year-old yellow shriveled-up plants out there on the plain. And Olle sat by the window on the sunlit nights and watched his neighbors. He moved from one room to the other. But preferably he stayed up on the roof of the haybarn building. From here he could see the ptarmigans scurry over the bluish green ice in the willow bushes at the mouth of a secondary river up there, but if this affectionately sounding cluck-cluck from a hen ptarmigan was heard over on the other side of the main river, a couple unmated males immediately raced over through the air, – well, they could likely be mated too for that matter – our Lord will know love is not just play and rapture and turf hut in the woods either … there is just as much a heart beneath the plumage that gets a fatal wound on such a spring morning in the woods.

New duck pairs and duck flocks come whistling down from the sky; the river and all backwaters and bays teem with ducks, and large flocks of wild geese cast shadows on the river and the plain yellow from shriveled-up plants when they sail their large, fat bodies over Helligskogen and hawk with a deep belly bass.

Good heavens, what a concert here in Helligskogen on these spring days.

Here are hundreds of ducks, and each of the three-four types have their own language, – here are thousands of small birds in the woods and on the river banks who themselves think they have the strongest throats in the whole world, and the wood grouse up on the wooded slope closes both its ears and eyes to all the world's dangers and has enough with its own game. Well, who doesn't? The male ptarmigan indeed doesn't have an ear for other sounds in the middle of all this noise than the female's cluck-cluck somewhere in the scrub and its own melancholy, love-sick laughter.

And the spring flood booms and rumbles through Helligskogen. Up there the two rivers rush together in white foamy rapids around a bare rock point under a high wooded slope, and their collected flood of water goes over all banks down here – the lower lying birch woods and willow groves above the plain stand in water – yes, along the foot of the slope a bay goes far in over the plain, so Olle for the moment lives on a peninsula. And here below the buildings the flood is just a couple meters beneath the riverbank.

All kinds of odds and ends and trees – which have plunged down together with the protruding edges of heather in that the flood has eaten its way into the sand walls beneath – sail with resisting roots and branches down the river.

After the breaking up of the ice some eight days ago there still lie huge ice floes built high up on the beaches, – then there was noise here, then there was the ice that turned up the great, roaring song.

Now the valley floor is mostly devoid of snow; but the plateaus around are still full of snow masses melting in the sun and south wind and sending yellow strips of plunging creeks and entire small rivers down over all the clefts in the mountainsides.

There is song here. There is noise here. There is sun and south wind here, and it's beginning to turn green on the sunlit slopes. There is morning joy here, there are thousands of throats quivering in wild exultation. The waters are singing here, nests are being built here.

Olle has a couple of nets in a backwater up there, and he has gotten quite a few grayling and trout; he has made himself a nice little raft. And when the flood has diminished and the water has cleared, the salmon throngs come hurrying up from the sea, – the roughly two hundred and fifty miles up here they wriggle their way in just a few days.

And the mountain lakes around are full of trout and the fat reddish white char. Here the grass grows thick and full on every open spot in the birch woods.

Here Aile will walk, beautiful and light and buxom, and God will bestow on them a whole little flock of little Olles and Ailes. They have several hundred reindeer in father-in-law Jauna Jauna's herd. On summer evenings they will sit here in the yard and wait for the cows hurrying home from the outlying fields to be milked – they hear the bells jingle in the birch woods up there. And Olle has a smithy and carpenter workshop, and he can, well, God only knows what he can do! He forges knives and makes sleds and sells them to the West Parish folks and to whomever. And he builds little boats for their children and to have up on the mountain lakes.

Here are foxes and otters and weasels, and what can't Aile sew of Sámi shoes and the like – leather goods are exported here from Helligskogen.

And here are no quarrelsome and repulsive neighbors and roués to gossip with Aile.

A person could be consumed with well-being and happiness in Helligskogen, and better one could not ask for.

Here is a church, here is the altar's sacrament and Christian burial to be had when the minister comes and the graveyard is consecrated.

But Olle still has long to live. He will hold school here in the winter. He will build several buildings; the mountain Sámi will be spared from sending their children down to the villages. And he will get used to preaching the word purely and chastely; he will sing; he will compose; he will cut out in wood, images of people and gods and animals; he will draw and paint – if he can! – ask, if he can! He will go to communion with morning joy in his chest.

A good place will Helligskogen become.

God grant him a long life!

But his dust will rest in the graveyard over there by the chapel. His children are married to mountain Sámi around here, and they will honor their father's memory, the memory of a good father who tried to live in a way he thought was most proper to live.

But one of them, the youngest one, the one named Jens after his grandfather will become a dentist. Dentist Jens Olsen. He will read his father's book about 'Cheerful Tenacity'; he will understand it cost the blessed departed a lot to gain the happiness that fell to his lot in Helligskogen.

… A wagtail trips around in the yard in the early morning hour, darts with some cheerful bounces into the air and settles down on the storehouse steps and peeks around the corner.

Suddenly the herd of hares grazing out on the plain disperses – it was as if someone had beat with a ladle down in a milk dish … a fox goes around and strikes down without mercy – duck- and wild goose flocks that have rested on the beaches below the rapids up there fly up into the air, – a couple foxes sneak away each with a fat duck in its jaws.

Here sail large eagles over Helligskogen; but when they dive down from their high spheres to fetch their allotted dish, – well, then one just says yes and amen to it.

Here are night owls in Helligskogen.

And here is a person who is used to remembering a sin that was beyond human power.

On the perilous passage among the mountains

One morning at the beginning of July Olle is sitting out in the yard and plucking a wild goose. Tomorrow he will finally tear himself loose and head down the valley.

... Lord Jesus – it's Aile! It is only Aile who walks like that – she is walking over the plain – this plain which has been his salvation and is so also now.

But Aile isn't walking the way she usually walks – she's walking sadly now, and Olle doesn't even ask himself what this might mean. They have contrived to remain here in the inland, and so it has dawned on them they have eaten from the forbidden fruit and they have tried to hide on the plateau, because they felt they had done something bad, and they were ashamed.

Olle heads out over the plain to meet her.

... He was right. Of course he was right. And he tried to console her as best he could – it was absolutely not anything to take so sadly, and when he kissed her, it was almost fatherly, and she received his kiss too as a pious consolation.

Olle roasted the goose and boiled coffee, while Aile lay and rested – poor little, fair Aile felt so lost, she couldn't manage to say anything. She fell asleep before Olle got the food ready, and Olle let her sleep it off.

She slept until late in the afternoon.

... When they had eaten and drunk coffee, she began to talk.

They hadn't come any farther than 20-25 miles northward when the females began to drop calves. They pitched camp by a mountain lake, in a little valley that led down to the big river.

They stayed there eight days; but there were still many females who had not dropped calves. Now, for that matter, they could just as well have continued on and taken breaks little by little. But it was as if they couldn't get around to leaving. There was always something in the way, and there was no one who said now they ought to see about leaving again. Well, Gudnel's kids were you know eager in the beginning to harp on their needing to go on. But it was as if no one listened to them, and then the little ones too forgot to speak about it.

… But one morning, it was such lovely sunshine and calm weather, father, Jauna Jauna, says sure enough they could just as well settle down where they were for the summer and the devil grappling with the long way northward, and the snow conditions had also gotten rather poor and would gradually get worse: the thawing of the ice on the lakes and rivers and the bare spots on the plateau would make it well-nigh impossible to make their way with the herd and the string.

Well, then *that* was said. And they all agreed on it. They had been a little taciturn of late without their being able to help it. But now, when Jauna Jauna had said it, it was as if the tongues were loosened on all of them, and that day they were maybe a little more cheerful than felt natural. Well, Jauna Jauna had even started to yoik – though it is a sin to yoik, and something devout people are not in the habit of doing.

… Now they stayed there. And they continued to lead devotions in the tent every Sunday morning as they had always done. Jauna Jauna read aloud the day's text and meditation in the Lutheran book of sermons, and both before and after they sang a hymn.

But one Sunday there were no devotions, and it would turn out there weren't any the next Sunday either. And the sincere satisfaction that had always reigned in the family had somehow been deluded away. It was impossible to conjure it up. Good grief, what was to be done? Well, they pretended to be ignorant of the situation. But that didn't help.

Father had become difficult, he did, he who had always been goodness itself. Yes, one time something terrible burst out of him – he cursed, he swore aloud that the devil could just as well condemn him; but Jauna Jauna was going to show he still was well within his rights.

… But afterwards Jauna Jauna had gone away and cried – Gudnel's oldest boy had seen grandfather sitting on a rock in the grove above the tent crying … And yet no Sunday devotions were held anymore.

Of course, they had tried to take comfort in not being discovered staying here inland the entire summer. But that wouldn't befit the consolation – on the contrary, it just made the whole thing worse.

Aile sat and cried a while. She was as honest and unostentatious as her very countenance.

But finally her father had dished it out what no one up to now had wanted to admit. The whole thing was Olle's fault. Jauna Jauna had even fallen into temptation by saying many coarse and unjust words about Olle. But then he had also been sort of relieved. The whole things was Olle's fault. Olle had cheered Jauna Jauna up with veiled and frivolous words; he hadn't only turned Aile's head, but also Gudnel and the old one … well, it was in any case Olle who had been the decisive factor. If he hadn't been here at Helligskogen, then this never would have happened to Jauna Jauna.

That blame Olle would more than willingly assume, so much the more as of course it wasn't his just as a joke. He wanted to be able to tolerate bearing it, – if it accordingly were to be discovered that … He would admit he had interpreted the law wrong for Jauna Jauna and managed to convince him it was neither a sin against God nor any punishable crime against the law, if the conditions made it necessary for him to have to settle down here inland for the summer.

The Jauna Jaunas alone wouldn't have been able to tolerate bearing it. Well, for as Aile said, how would they be able to meet in the village and look people in the eyes after this. The Jauna Jaunas have done this – this only poorer people would hit on doing.

Aile had to sob!

No, the fault was solely Olle's. Good heavens, Aile naturally didn't insist on it. But only now did it dawn on Olle what he actually had committed. He had been guilty in the moral ruin of a thoroughly good and respectable family – well, if one began to think about the scope of this it was quite dismaying. What else had been his simple duty than to point out to Jauna Jauna the seriously critical in embarking on this experiment. He had on the contrary encouraged him, and the women had naturally pushed it. Olle had in frivolous irrresponsibility struggled with his influence on these three innocent Sámi women here in the wilderness – without the slightest thought of how he thereby was putting an entire family's happiness at risk.

… Father had himself a couple times been on the way down to Olle, Aile related further; but he hadn't been able to go all the way. He had even stood up there on the mountainside escarpment and watched Olle go and putter around down here. Yes, for he had happened to think it would be best to hide it from Olle too … what wouldn't Olle think about the Jauna Jaunas after this?

Then he wouldn't have anything to do with Aile any more.

But if they really confided in Olle – and that were to be discovered all the same afterwards? – merciful God, how all ways out were hopeless! And originally they had all quietly looked forward to being able to be together with Olle here at Helligskogen.

… Well, then there was still nothing other to do than take a chance in God's name – Aile would have to take the difficult road to Helligskogen. She too had been on the verge of turning back again. No, she couldn't say what she had gone through during her hike here the previous night and this morning.

Aile's account had such a sad and shocking effect on Olle that at the moment he couldn't have anything else in his thoughts than to try to comfort her as best he could – he just sat there and held her lovingly in to himself and let her relate.

… But Aile had kept quiet again and again; there was something she was unable to find an outlet for. And now she again remains silent, and keeps quiet for a long time. Finally, she says afraid and searching for words:

"Father was gone an entire day recently" … "He had been up on a large ridge, west of our camp. We are surely not alone here in the interior," he said when later in the night he came back again.

Olle gave a start – he got up.

"Well, for father had seen reindeer on a mountain farther to the west. And it couldn't be wild reindeer, for there are no wild reindeer up here. Well, father thought he had seen smoke too."

"And who might it be?" asks Olle; he knows himself he is asking as a bluff.

"Well, father believed … well, we all believe … Aile looks around groping and resigned … well, that it maybe is the Saivos."

"Nor is there any doubt about it," Olle says.

And now Aile burst into tears again.

For just think if the Saivos were to discover the Jauna Jaunas too had stayed here in the interior.

Olle said nothing; he just kept quiet. But he had been aroused from the depression Aile's report up to now had held him in … Is that so, Saivos had also remained in here. See, that was something else. It almost overshadowed this business with Jauna Jaunas.

No, old Saivo certainly didn't go into the wilderness and be tormented by remorse at being stuck here, – by speculations as to what extent this was a sin against God and against the law. That much Olle had seen that time the original with this magpie miracle broke out.

Olle didn't feel tempted to have any compassion for him. For Saivo it was quite surely just a solace and carousing to commit this prank. And he was probably hardly even capable of feeling inconvenienced by having broken with God and his earlier godfearing life. It was probably only now, he thought, he had settled back into the old grooves again; now he could revel in his old magpie delights – better late than never; the old man would still be able to steal reindeer and holler and bellow and drink brandy in a farmyard in the west village and swear with an apoplectic bloodshot hawk face he was the richest and most respected man in the county – and he could still be more devout than anyone – just wait!

"… But what has your father thought of doing now?" Olle asks.

"Thought of doing … well, if only one knew what one had to do. Start to head north now was out of the question – they could come upon travelers on the way, and and then it would just be making matters worse. But Jauna Jauna had talked about it maybe being best to move over to the south side of the valley … then they could in any case be somewhat assured the Saivos wouldn't get wind of them."

Yes, there was of course always a good way out, Olle thought. Just the thought Saivo should get the upper hand on Jauna Jauna, – seemed to him like something revolting! … How had they made their entry here in Helligskogen at Easter? The son, Piera, and the others, well, they came – they were going to come at full speed, pretentious in all their magpie splendor, boisterous, yoiking – and then came, was going to come old Saivo, the old miracle, driving meekly – as befits a believer, a true

Christian, the West Parish's renowned holy miracle … and the meek, old monster climbed from the sled, looked around and blessed the entire gathered congregation in Helligskogen … "*Ipmil ráfi buohkaidi!*[34] God's peace be with you all!"

May old rotgut fink Erik take Olle, if it should happen Saivo were to get the better of Jauna Jauna!

The thought of this had such a terrible effect on Olle the vital spirits awoke immediately … yes, this he would probably manage – the hell with going down to the village for the time being – that could be put off until sometime in August … then he would go down and get the boat and the cow and bull and a couple people to help him break ground.

Aile too had perked up before she knew it. They were sitting out on the riverbank this warm July evening and looking at the ducks in the river which had now gone down and turned clear. The white sand edges had emerged, and the big rapids up there where the two rivers meet around a sloping rock point under a high pine hillside had gotten smaller and sparkled in the evening sun. Olle sat and talked about the two slender, small riverboats he was going to build, and their boys were going to pole them up the rapids up there to fish salmon …

But more seriously he and Aile were now agreed when they had gotten the herd and the family safely over onto the south side of the valley, then Aile was going to be here with Olle. They were going to fish salmon in the river and trout in the mountain lakes, and in August they were going to begin with the 'haying' – there were open spots here in the birch woods along the river where extremely thick, fine grass was growing.

And they walk and look at what Olle has done out on the plain. He had burnt and scorched large strips of heather and thick, yellow, old grass, – the ashes had been lying there like a glistening lead carpet; the spring rain had sunk down into the soil and now fine grass was beginning to grow.

"Just think, it's already full summer down here in the valley," Aile says, and she looks at the deciduous trees along the river, and at the little flowers on the grassy hills.

"Look, here is *sáhpan biellu*,"[35] – she always has her own names for the flowers; but there are many flowers she doesn't know, – she just calls them *hearva rássi*, showy grass. They walk around the buldings, and there too Olle has burned out heather and all the old grass so it has turned into a beautiful meadow around. And all sorts of lumber stands raised up against the barn walls – Olle had also as a child had a true passion for lumber, and when last spring he was walking in the woods he could almost not make his way – there a birch which could be made into excellent sled runners, – there a pine root for boat ribs … and he had stood in the yard and

---

[34] May God's peace be with all of you!
[35] *Sáhpan biellu* – Nor. *musebjelle*, Eng. harebell – *Campanula rotundifolia*.

cut shavings from and chewed bark. And when fresh, hewed pieces of birch lay and smelled up on the hearth, then it felt cozy here in Helligskogen.

The scrubbed rooms sparkled, and the human voices sounded so airy and summery in there, – yes, how lovely and refreshing it was to hear voices again! Olle who otherwise had had to speak alone, had in spring, strangely enough in the first uneasy feelings of loneliness, sudddenly gotten an idea which became a superstition with him: he wasn't going to say anything out loud – he could whisper, but nothing more. And he had gone around whispering to himself all this time he had been here alone.

"Have you walked around here whispering to yourself?" – and Aile laughed and forgot all her worries.

Now all fright had disappeared. They stood close to each other, and the female aroma suddenly took his strength away …

On the exchange of goods and merchandise without money

The day after, they went over the wooded hillsides and north to Jauna Jauna's camp.

And already the following night Jauna Jauna and family set to work with the migration over the valley, some 12 miles below Helligskogen. Olle was along, and he made a large and solid raft to ferry people and tents and all the rest over the river.

The new camp they pitched by a mountain lake near the Finnish border, about twenty miles south of Helligskogen.

Now Jauna Jauna was elated again, and he and Olle sat one evening up on a ridge above the tents. The lake below lay mirrorlike in the evening sun, surrounded by rush- and birch- and willow bushes, and on the level plateaus around swelled reindeer moss plump and greenish yellow between crowberry heather and small scrubs of dwarf birch – here the reindeer who had no qualms of conscience to carry along could sink down in great well-being. They barely bothered to graze now. But they had surely lived well over there on the north side of the valley too, – their antlers were growing large and nice; but they were still covered by the black, downy haired skin. Their antlers itch during growth; the reindeer must rub them against the trees or scratch them first with the one back leg then with the other, and during this occupation, the Sámi claim, the reindeer take care the antlers and branches on them get the right, resplendent shape. The new hair on the animals was still quite short and black, and on the calves the yellowish, soft as down tone had started to darken.

Down there the smoke from the fire outside the tents was blue and straight up into the air, and Jauna Jauna and Olle could hear Gudnel's and Little-Andi's kids playing and making noise down there by the lake.

"Well, it's been bad for us during this time, Olle," Jauna Jauna says, "I've had to think about a lot which I didn't need to think about before. It is as if the world has shown its troublesome side to all of us – well, mostly to me. It is strange for someone who has the responsibility. I feel most sorry for the children, Gudnel's children. Until now we always lived happily, and we had nothing to hide from anyone or needed to be ashamed of. And then the children would be witness to our getting involved in something we had to be ashamed of and had to try to hide from others. Yes, the little ones saw it to be sure; they understood it so very well, especially the oldest boy. They stood face to face with sin, poor little ones. They will never again be able to forget this. They noticed everything; they listened and understood every little hint. And suffered in the same way as the rest of us … Maybe we grownups haven't been like this before God's eyes that we could live through – although we have been believers. But it is my hope God for his son's sake will forgive us and purge us from this depravity. For now I have somehow realized all this. We are allowed to use the mountain plateaus in here, but it is not our land such that we own it – we move over a large land, and we cannot own all the places we come to. The land is the state's. And there must be laws and a good system if the people are not going to destroy common land and property for each other."

"… But what do you say about Saivo, Olle? Now, I of course am no better than he in this case. But it is so he fell into sin in such a bad way … so I don't know, – I somehow have no faith in him being able to repent his sin."

*   *

*

Aile is mostly down with Olle in Helligskogen. That was the upshot.

Now Olle has told her about Agnete and how it happened they had been pulled away from each other. It was a new and strange world that opened up for Aile here. It occupied her thoughts continually – not even in dreams could she avoid it. If they sat and talked about their own everyday concerns, she could suddenly turn silent and sit and look self-sacrificing.

But gradually she disclosed it wasn't so strange for her any more. Little questions, little conjectures she came out with, let it be apparent in spite of all the distance both in the one and the other sense, a living image of the whole thing had formed.

… One day Olle says to her it is after all an irresponsible lack of caution for her to stay down here: there was no guarantee Saivos weren't glancing down into Helligskogen from up on the steep mountain slope – Olle said it out of a genuine concern for the Jauna Jaunas not being discovered by Saivos.

She gave a start.

In the evening the same day Jauna Jauna shouted from the other side of the river. Yes, Jauna Jauna had also come to the same thought as Olle.

And they had also taken a trip down there to where they had moved the herd over. They hid the raft, and the strong downpour in recent days had mostly smoothed out the tracks on the riverbanks from the herd – thanks to smooth rock on both sides of this place the remains of the tracks couldn't be seen very well from the river – if someone were to come poling up.

… But Olle hadn't been alone many days before he again heard someone calling carefully over on the other side – it was already late in the evening.

No, Aile didn't think it was so dangerous if she visited him a few nights.

Often she stayed over until the next night; but then she stayed inside the whole day.

There was no doubt she had begun to be fearful that Olle would get time to think about other things while she was away – such deliberations in free solitude, after one has come out on top can lead to so much.

She always came bathed and in her finest costume, the one of the red striped quilted cloth which hung so seductively light out over her young, sumptuously buxom chest. Her Sámi boots were small and pretty, and the ties around the shanks were always wrapped with the greatest care. And inside she went around with her light golden hair hanging loose, so pure in her open blue-eyed countenance, unostentatious and pure in her soul too when desire burned most intensely in her young, strongly awakened senses.

But when they seemed to be getting along best, she could suddenly succumb to one or other thought that made her uneasy, and she took refuge in him and said she felt afraid.

On the duck family

He had ferried Aile across the river during the night. And the same morning while he is standing out on the riverbank and gathering dirt out of a fishnet he had just hung up on scaffolding, he suddenly becomes aware of someone coming poling up the river, along the shore with the small pebbles on this side.

It is three boats, one after the other; they are poled two and two by two slender men in white shirts with white belts around the waist and in white homespun pants. They swing their 18-foot-long, white poling sticks in time and easily. Everything shines in the morning sun; the reddish glistening tarred boats, the gunwale under the high, extended prows and the sparkling sharp waves spread out over the strong river current and wash up against the shore with the small pebbles.

Oh, how Olle recognized this sight – how it made his proud, happy childhood memories flare up!

It was the east village folks, folks from Erki Lemik Issak's village – they were probably out fishing salmon and had poled the 90 miles up here – the salmon, the rapids, the waterfalls had urged them up – a pleasure- and fishing trip, enjoyment such as pushing a boat up the current, so to speak, just steering it up between the rocks the waterfall rapids pour over … and a weakling it was whose poling stick wasn't new and white and 18 feet long.

Then they could at the same time say hello to Olle, see the new chapel, fish more salmon up in the two rivers – a pleasure- and a useful trip …

The party people – party at the bonfires on the riverbank, and when the salmon net in the morning hours drives down toward the barrier, and a dozen boats drive along as buoys, and all thirty, right from the sheet pullers on the beaches, are busy heaping libelous ditties on each other and the latest nonsense about Tom, Dick and Harry. And party and everlasting fun it was, when with the spring flood they went down the river with their small log rafts, – the ever humor-filled spectacle followed their horse caravans during the winter, – wherever they came, it turned into fun. These blue-eyed and slender river people are the only ones up there who really have gotten their stamp from the sunlit nights, from the white sandbanks, from the deciduous trees along the river promontories, from the pine slopes around, from the country's most beautiful spot which the east village down there and its environs are.

But *the way* – and *the way* also on the boats that now come whizzing up the stubborn current down there as if they were drifting at full sail, – it was created by an *Anáraš*,[36] by the long deceased, black-eyed and broad-shouldered village chieftain, the east village's last Mongol.

What has otherwise become of the small black-eyed people, only our Lord knows. Here in the valley they no longer existed, in any case as isolated types – the last fullblooded *Anáraš* was probably he who was now standing here on the river sand bluff – with his hands squeezed on the wet net and with his eyes fastened on the sight below … well, let the dead bury their dead. They have nevertheless been here once and left the blue-eyed and hawk faces *a way* – also *that way* only shreds of which are found in the West Parishes' magpies and in the turf huts down by the fjords.

… Now Olle can hear the gunwale and the pole shafts beat against the gunwale.

—

… Yes, it was Juhaš, happy Juhaš, and then it was Andi Piera and Ommuk Nilas, Lemik Lemik's son, Siri Andaras and Dullerova Jussa.

They had mail for Olle – a single letter, and he refrained from opening it, – although his heart started to throb when he put it aside … 'Cheerful tenacity' …

Yes, Olle knew them, everybody, and the first day was entirely talked away – Olle of course didn't have the least idea of what had happened in this world since he in March left the marketplace by one of the fjords to the west.

Of course, they had already heard about all the remarkable things that had happened here at Easter – about Bittoš Hansa and about that dreadful, that old, Christian Saivo suddenly possessed by the devil. That had been in the newspapers also, and now the sheriff too had thought about taking a trip up here, but when he heard Juhaš and the others were going up, he wanted to wait to hear what they had to tell. For it had seemed rather strange too that Olle hadn't come down to the village, but had given himself over to staying here alone. Well, that had frankly speaking looked suspicious.

As was their custom down there Juhaš and the others properly examined the chapel painstakingly to see how it was built – besides the Swede a few others from the east village had helped build it. And Juhaš and the others could see who had worked on that wall, who on the other – they could tell it by the cut of the axe.

And they lay in the sun on the grassy hill out there on the river sand bluff and talked about everything between heaven and earth.

"Is that so, Saivo Piera went out the door hiccuping, and Hoammá Čuonja sat there with the wedding gifts on her lap," and Juhaš' long face with the long double incisors laughed up toward the sky.

---

[36] *Anáraš* – resident of Enare.

"And here went *Anáraččat* and *Hoammát* and West Parish folks cleaned and in only cold hide fur coats and froze to death," Juhaš squirmed with laughter and moaned because it was both a sin and shameful to laugh at it.

"And the herder lost Bittoš Hansa's body, and you couldn't find it," – now Juhaš was serious, "and so Bittoš Hansa's life ended in that manner" – Juhaš sat serious and looked straight in front of himself; but then some red spots began to form on his face … "Is that so, he lost both his life and the sled – "… may heaven forgive Juhaš his sin," Juhaš broke into laughter, and they kept their hands on their stomachs and laughed.

Well, in any case they didn't know anything about further consequences of the events at Easter … that Olle had neighbors, law breakers up here during the summer – up here in the great wilderness.

Olle got them involved in the clearing effort, and in the course of three days there was a large and promising, newly cleared piece of ground above the plain, where it looked most fertile, and now large piles of birch and willow and roots lay on the dug up ground. They were real strong men at clearing, and the whole thing had taken place during the same, ever humor-filled racket that accompanied them everywhere, – they were of course party folks from the valley of the sunlit nights. And in the morning hours they 'steered' their boats higher up the waterfall rapids to fish for salmon in deep pools up above.

"And Erki Lemik Issak's son hasn't come along with you up here," Olle says.

"No," says Juhaš, "for there doesn't exist the belt that can hold the pleats on his costume in the right order on such trips as this one. Pole the few miles up to the summer dairy on a Saturday, that can be done without his garb getting out of or-der; but otherwise we mostly see him strolling on the meadow paths at home now during the summer when the meadows and the huts are clean and fine."

"And then he is going to be the son-in-law of Juhaš," Siri Andaras says.

"Well, damnation," Juhaš laughs, "if there is going to be a son-in-law, then it'll be! Erki Lemik Issak's son so to speak is going to be in a picture frame in our attic room."

"And you don't want to go down with us?"

No, Olle didn't want to, for many weighty reasons. Now above all he wanted to clear more land. But in the fall, then …

Well, they had their own ideas about Olle; they had probably heard something or other, how things had gone for him in this world. They just didn't know that Olle had people here he couldn't leave to himself.

*   *
*

And now they were all gone. The magpie folks in a sort of second generation … but *the way* they had gotten from an *Anáraš*, from Olle's father.

Now Olle was alone; now he opened the letter, the most difficult thing he had done here at Helligskogen.

— —

… Well, now I have told you. And now I feel relieved. It's bad enough to be plagued by guilt, but a thousand times worse to be plagued by innocence – the way you have done. Yes, for I know, dear Olle, what you said to me that night, that terrible night, when you opened the window and closed it again and let me go my way, – that you have since considered a sin beyond one's ability … just because you knew, thought you knew, you had done this to an innocent one – an innocent one who loved you, in spite of everything, and whom you in spite of everything still loved … now you know accordingly I wasn't innocent. You knew nothing you couldn't know; you had at that point in time, when the bad ignited in you, absolutely no real suspicion; you just began to suspect, apparently without any reason whatsoever. But you suspected correctly, Olle; you began to suspect precisely at the right moment. Where the impulse originated, see, that probably belongs to those riddles, from what I hear, we continually have to trudge through. But now you can take comfort your action towards me has not been a sin beyond one's ability. Well, for it is probably immaterial to you now whether I was guilty or not guilty, – just that you can be convinced that the act you haven't been able to forgive yourself for, however was fair, justified.

Whether I myself feel regret? Certainly I regretted it at the time and did penance – also as a matter of fact – well, you understand. And I feel sorry perhaps now every so often; but one cannot feel sorry one's entire life.

Now, in spite of everything I want finally to send you a fond greeting, and I hope in spite of everything you construe as it is meant. Well, for my greeting to you is sincere enough, Olle.

Agnete

— —

It's late in the afternoon, and Olle is still going and shuffling in the doors, closes one door and goes in from another door. This he has indeed done the entire day … "Lies! – Lies, Agnete!" … but one day it had to happen that also you saw yourself forced to fence yourself in with cheerful tenacity. Good grief, how I forgive you your lie! Once in our lives we have to walk in the strait jacket of cheerful tenacity.

Good grief, how I forgive you your lie!

We have to have something to hibernate in.

On wolves and their fierceness

Say it – believe it at the moment … it was just something she had come up with at a desperate and bad time … say it … but get it gently to sit fast … for many days Olle struggled with an uncontrollable urge to leave and say farewell to Helligskogen to refresh himself in the final conviction that she wasn't only slandering herself; but that it also was true!

But he remained where he was. Driven to that by God knows what instinct. Now when all is said and done it was probably a sort of a self-preservation inclination which in spite of everything got him to try to tighten his grip on this house in Helligskogen and refrain from challenging the dead – truth's ghosts.

Out in the yard a tame gosling plods around and eats grass the livelong day. It has now begun to get feathers and wings; but the pouches are still bare and bluish and there are still parts of the brownish yellow down sticking out. She's called the administrator. In the morning she usually takes a trip down to the river, turns somersaults down the steep sand dune, but pretends to be ignorant of the situation and sways from side to side over the pebbles down to the river edge, pours water into herself, and she is in good company; she begins to swim out, yes, she's really in her element, she gives a demonstration of swimming- and diving arts only a goose can do – a pure apparition doing somersaults under the water surface. Then she stops and smartens up and cares for herself on the shore, catches sight of Olle up on the river sand bluff, lets out a howl of joy and comes bounding up the hill with bloated wings and whinnies up toward Olle with her good, solid look.

Well done, little one, well done, and they go together into the living room to get something good, a piece of bread or such.

*   *
*

Then one evening Olle hears the little shout – and there sits Aile on the smooth rock on the other side, right under Wolf Mountain. And Olle rows over with the raft.

Yes, Aile had seen the people come poling up the river that morning; it was while she was on the way back. And both she and Jauna Jauna and Gudnel had been down on Wolf Mountain to look at them, while they were walking around here and shuffling between the living room and the boats down on the river bank. It had been so strange to see other people again – had one only been able to go down and talk with them, they had all said.

… They have eaten and drunk coffee, and now they are sitting again at Olle's regular place out on the river sand bluff – no, one can never get tired of seeing the river run, see the rapids in the evening sun up there – see the river decrease and darken down there as it bumps against the river promontory with lush deciduous trees and bends to the left, around a sand ridge sticking out.

That something had happened to Olle Aile had seen as soon as he came ashore over there. And now they were sitting here on the river sand bluff, and she was looking at him from the side; she had a feeling it was just this way a person had to look when flood or lightning from the sky or fire and ashes from the earth's interior had made an end of everything he had built up in his life, everything he had got to grow and everything he had become one with. There is nothing to do about that, and one somehow is unable to have confidence something in this world can still compensate for the loss.

… She had given him reason to notice the warmth, but he had been as if poisoned – a woman's warmth touches a man in vain who lies in fever; the fever paralyzes the man in every respect. And Aile couldn't bring herself to interrogate him – good grief, what good would that have done! But it was probably so it should end now …

"… I want to go home," Aile says suddenly; they have sat silently a while.

"You want to go home now?" – Olle somehow seems to wake up.

"Yes, You must row me over."

Olle saw she meant it, and at the moment this also appeared unimportant to him. Yes, it was as if he found a sort of solace, a torrential spiritual delight in letting her go.

"Well, as you wish. You want to go over right away?"

"Yes," and now Aile too had become severe in her face and voice. She had gotten up and stood there beautiful and proud and wounded.

— —

No, he didn't row her over this evening.

And the days passed.

Aile didn't know herself what she was for Olle at this time. She saw to be sure he was beginning to be livelier from day to day, and she understood too there was a reason he was trying to cling to her, wanted somehow to seek shelter for his mind in her. But what this cost Olle of self-conquest and what sort of confounded and dark world he was struggling against, and that at times he literally felt squeezed between life and death, that was something she couldn't get to know herself.

They cut hay at the open spots in the birch woods above the plain and along the river. They fished in the river and in the mountain lakes near Jauna Jauna's camp. But the administrator kept steadfastly to the buildings, and when Olle again appeared, she was beside herself with joy; she was almost just as smart as a dog, well, not far from it, she knew how to put on airs, in any case, she wagged her tail when she saw Olle busy making a delicious porridge for her. But good grief, how fat she was!

Aile no longer cared she was running a risk of being seen by some of the Saivos. Nor did the others either. For now Jauna Jauna had made a serious decision: he was going to report himself as an offender. He strongly had in mind to go down to the village already now during the summer; it was best to get it done the sooner the better.

However that may be: the Jauna Jaunas were again on the way to becoming the happy family they had always been. And now they had also so to speak personally learned to recognize sin – if they ever were to do penance for it, then it would still be lovely to be alive. A blot on their name they had no doubt gotten, a blot that couldn't be washed off, in any case not face to face with their fellow humans. Yes, Olle could be right: it always costs a sacrifice to come a step closer to God and learn to know one's own frailty.

And one Saturday afternoon they all turned up, the herders too, down here in Helligskogen, and Sunday Olle led devotions in the chapel for the first time since last spring. However, they didn't venture to ring the bell. The bell sound could be heard far across the plateau, and one shouldn't tempt fate and the Saivos more then necessary. After devotions Jauna Jauna came out with an expression of his feelings: the one who had also been able to go to the altar – well, first confess his sins with remorse and the desire to be born again and then eat of the Lord's bread and drink of his blood.

*   *

*

Olle had little by little become a passive instrument in Aile's hand; he discovered it himself too; it was no longer just a sensual abandonment, no longer just Aile's young, beautiful body and her strongly open lust for life that had a distracting effect on him and got him, in any case in part, to conquer the consequences of the poisoning the letter had caused. No, also Aile herself noticed she had become something more for him, and that not only feigned or from ulterior motives. She had become a human being for him, she thought; he had become so full of confidence, and what is more, she seemed to understand she now had begun to comprehend her life here at Helligskogen seriously; it had somehow become another hold on him.

Aile actually was unable to find an outlet for this surplus feeling of happiness. She teased Olle, she pampered him – yes, so completely had she encircled him she now could afford to think about other people and longed to be able to display herself and her happiness.

*   *

*

… It was already a good ways into August. And again the starry sky arched over Helligskogen in the evening and at night. During the day the air is sort of polished – one can see so infinitely far; one can see the individual trees on the most distant mountainside ridge; one can see birds resting on a smooth rock way up at the rapids.

… Olle didn't notice it the first couple of times; but when it happened more and more often that Aile made errands for herself to the chapel, well, she on the whole liked to show herself out on the plain, then he of course couldn't avoid taking note of it. And if he had only taken note of it, then … She pretended she was eating crow-berries out there, she was especially fond of doing it in the evening. One time Olle seemed to see precisely that she was standing and listening out there and keeping an eye on the wooded hill that adjoins the plain. His eyes grew dim; he couldn't help it, but summoned a sheer superhuman force not to express anything.

One evening she says the net they had hung up in the morning up there by the side river's mouth, had fallen down. It couldn't lie there; she would go and hang it up.

"Yes, do it," Olle said; he said it so obviously indifferent, while she stood and shaped a frame piece. And just as matter of course Aile set out upward, along the river sand bluff. It had already begun to grow dark. A few minutes later Olle hurries with back bent out over the plain, in another direction, goes up the mountainside ridge, runs into the pine barren, now up toward the side river. He catches sight of Aile; she still hasn't reached the net – and what was she going to do with the net? – It's hanging there. She stands outside on the river sand bluff, in such a way she is seen here from the mountainside; she goes back and forth and again stands still and sort of listens.

Olle has hidden himself behind a large pine. Should he – shouldn't he?
"Hey, hey!"
Aile straightens up, stands immovably still and stares up at the wooded slope.
"Hey, hey," sounds from the wooded slope.
Aile takes a couple steps forward. Long silence.
"Hey, hey!"
"Hey, hey!" Aile answers with a tremblingly weak voice.
"Is it you, Aile?"
"Yes … Is it you, Piera?"
"Yes. Come up here."
And Aile heads up the hill. It is almost completely dark.
"Where are you?"
"Here."
And she walks in the direction the voice is heard. Now she has become almost calm; it is of course Piera's voice. And suddenly she stands in fromt of Olle, gives a shriek, sobs, moans, but cannot get out a word – he stands there as quiet as a spectre.

"Come now, Aile," he says in a hoarse voice and smiles, "come, let's flee, and the hell with Olle!"

And he embraces her.

"You want to be with me, isn't that so? Well, we'll lie down here, Aile."

He presses her down and pretends he is preparing everything.

Aile lies there helpless and in a demented terror; she stares into his eyes; his face, glowing, burns with a silent threat.

"Don't kill me, Olle, don't kill me," trembles out of her mouth.

He doesn't say a word; he just grasps her by the legs and drags her backwards. Her costume slides upward, and her bare back tears and scrapes against heather and dry, hard sprigs.

"Don't kill me, Olle," she shrieks heart-rendingly loud.

"Be quiet, damn it," he bellows, "I'll do what I want"; he grabs her by the shoulder and pulls her up, and the blows ring in her ears, while he yells out the most horrible oaths, and while she gasps for air and screams in mortal dread.

"Olle, may I say something …"

"No, you'll manage best by saying nothing," and he again raises his hand for a blow.

"I'm not in love with anyone but you"; she crouches down.

"I will advise you not to appear at my place any more."

And with that he left.

"May I speak to you, Olle?"

He stops abruptly. Aile stops too, but at a distance, afraid and shaking.

"It was just because I thought it could have been pleasant to talk to Piera. I'm not in love with anyone but you, Olle. But I think it could have been nice to talk to Piera. You must believe me, Olle. He of course didn't dare appear before you."

"You will not follow me a step more. I will advise you not to do it, Aile. You wanted it this way yourself, and you will find out … be quiet, just be quiet …"

And he takes the way homeward.

… Oh, how he was happy he had been able to discover the whole thing; yes, at this moment he felt he would have been disappointed if it had turned out Aile really had just had an ordinary honest errand up here.

He lies in his bed in the small side room. Maybe the two had arranged the whole thing last spring. They had agreed to deceive their respective parents into staying behind here. No more than a hint of that was needed.

… Olle finds himself walking on the floor. It is dark; but the sky is clear, and there is a white mist over the river, and a few streaks of mist drift in over the plain too. Suddenly he tears open the window, nervously and hastily as if it was a matter of saving himself from being choked … he sees the chapel's white painted contours in the dark.

"Ho, ho, you over there under the sand hills! You are certainly mistaken, you don't live on Christian ground, so much as you know it. Try to come over the mountain or down the valley; you'll surely find a proper graveyard on the way."

A September day in sun and calm; it's quite a day. The first snowfall occurred here already at the end of August; the snow remained overnight, but it disappeared again the following day, and a couple days later it had also disappeared from the distant, bare mountain ridges on the south side of the western valley district up there which one could see here from Helligskogen when one walked a little farther northward on the plain.

Aile still has a couple scars on her face, and she'll probably have them for the rest of her life. To those close to her she had said she hurt herself during a fall – she had rolled so badly down a smooth rock down by the river. And she had asked Olle for permission to come down to him still so the others wouldn't find out what had happened between them.

And they tried to be together as best they could.

They have cured quite a lot of fish, both salmon and trout and char; the river and the mountain lakes have been teeming this year. And they have hundreds of small, pretty, rounded piles of reindeer moss up on the level mountain plateaus, and the piles have birch switches stuck through them to make them stable. When they freeze, Aile and Olle will force them together into small mounds – and then drive all the moss down when there are good snow conditions. It had been a great lack for the mountain Sámi last winter that there hadn't been a *limpu*[37] to obtain here; they always had to go to the woods with the animals. Olle had thought of asking thirty øre for a *limpu*; there could be cash from it also, and not so little either.

* *

*

A September day in sun and calm; it's quite a day, – when it begins with the sunrise over dewy frozen fields and woods and mountains. The ice shines mirror-like over the ponds and in the calm waves in the river.

But the wild goose wedges sailing over Helligskogen in the early morning hours already sparkle in the sun's gleam up there.

Now the inordinately fat administrator is at a loss. She stares with ill yearning eyes up toward the sky, howls so it is almost painful to hear, and half flying she goes

---

[37] Clump.

back and forth over the yard. But leave this yard and these buildings – she would really have to scratch her head.

Just for fun Olle wrote one day a little note to Samuel Tønnesen, Holmestrand, and attached it to the foot of the administrator and tossed her high up in the air – she sailed away a bit, but sank slowly down again and came running back at full speed with played out wings.

Olle lay during the night and had nightmares, dreamt the administrator stuck her head up in his face and asked spitting but gently as well: was it Samuel Tønnessen, Holmestrand who was supposed to get the letter?

And when he just then awakened, he heard a tremendous wild goose racket; he looked out the window; the flock was high up under the sky, and he saw the administrator hovering over the river; she hawked with all her strength – it was as if she was imploring the others she for God's sake had to come along. And higher and higher she climbed – until she got Wolf Mountain over there beneath herself.

*   *

*

Already by the middle of September it had become full winter here; the river had calmed down; only the rapids above still remained open. The Jauna Jaunas could now travel on winter snow conditions between the camp and Helligskogen, and Gudnel's and Little-Andi's kids were sincerely delighted to be able to ride in the sled again; they seemed long since to have forgotten the sin's bewitching and unpleasant ghosts from last spring when they had still been here in the countryside.

But one day the end of the snow and unpleasant weather sets in, and the evening of the same day, while it is growing dark, Olle sees a shabby, wet man come trudging up the plain, along the river high bluff. It wasn't difficult for Olle to see it was a Sámi farmer from the East Parish.

Without a serious errand one doesn't walk the 90 miles up here, and that at this time of the year; the conditions were neither fish nor foul.

Olle couldn't help it; he felt anxious.

The man, Anda Juoksa,[38] had hardly come into the yard and taken Olle by the hand before he explained himself. He had a letter for Olle, and while he is busy pulling this and that up from the the chest of his costume, up from the large, flowing space the tucked up costume forms above the belt, to find the letter, he says along with the letter had come a request to the postmaster to see to it the letter was delivered without delay no matter what it cost.

— —

… Olle spends this night awake in his room.

Up one page and down the next she had written down again the same thing and in a way tried to make inquiries and explain why she had been able to hit on slander-

---

[38] Josef Andersen. Juoksa, really a nickname instead of Jovsset, Josef. Juoksa may also mean a bow.

ing herself with the dreadful. But, she says, had it really been the case – well, what she related in her last letter to Olle, then it would probably not have been dreadful. For if she really had been able to do it, that is, be unfaithful to him, then of course everything would have been different from beginning to end, and then it wouldn't have been dreadful. But then she wouldn't, she writes, be herself, and Olle wouldn't have been Olle; the entire thing would have been a reality outside themselves.

"But now I am Agnete, and you are Olle, and our life together fell apart in the way it did." — — Then I heard you had traveled up there, and it was as if not until then did I feel I had lost you in earnest. Only then was I really attacked by this feeling of loneliness which since, with many small interruptions, has stuck to me. Until then I had mostly thought only good about you, Olle, that is, I was always capable of understanding you and forgiving you, even when you in others' eyes were an inhuman person towards me. And when you then seriously had gotten sick, I was sincerely happy at being able to know inwardly I to the end had tried to extend a hand to you as best I could. That after what had befallen me that night, that terrible night, I was unable to get myself to go in to you at the hospital, you can't reproach me for that, Olle. I had suffered an insult beyond means. If you had hit me, if you had been a thousand times rougher and harder against me in another way, I still think I could have forgiven you. But you chose the one way to turn me away. It was too much for me, Olle – even when I got to find out you had just been a defenseless offer for a furtive illness.

… Then the feeling of emptiness came over me as said. I began to think only of myself. I began to be addicted to the idée fixe –, you had just gotten ill because you hated me, that I had only gone from defeat to defeat – that you simply had thrown me away without reason – because in a way you were unable to endure me any more. Oh, Olle, you should only know! … I could burn, I was ready to be suffocated by a humiliating feeling sitting far up in my throat.

Then – then it was I fell back on the desperate way out of slandering myself with the dreadful – yes, there was even a time I sort of felt conscience-stricken.

… Too late it dawned on me what I had done … Dear Olle, I was at one time your little girl. And now I want to ask you to try to believe I did it at a time when I felt divested of everything in this world, divested down to the root of the heart. Couldn't we meet, Olle? – some place or other up there. No, you say. But why not? Can't you at any rate think a little about it?

But one thing you must know: without this doomed act of mine I would never have been able to extend a hand to you in this life. For that night, Olle …

I don't doubt you will believe in my innocence. But Agnete who was once your little girl, asks you to believe she acted poorly against her will when she wrote the letter."

On the many different types of bird, and the
distinction between them

A large gathering was here at Helligskogen the first Sunday in Advent.
From everywhere sled roads led to the yard. Already early in the morning candles were burning in the chapel, and a blue smoke curled round, pleasant curves right up into the calm, frosty clear air. Likewise from the house and the barn building; for some had to settle down in the cow barn too.

And someone was constantly riding down to the river with the water tub where there was a large, round hole in the ice; the state's well over by the northern end of the hay barn building had not become really usable yet.

The ministers and sheriffs from both the parishes had been entrusted with the small side room; Olle had temporarily installed himself in the small attic room a little stairstep led up to from the hall.

There were a good deal more people here now than at Easter, both of *Anáraččat* and West Parish folks and East Parish folks and *Hoammát* and the Swedish knit caps. And now all the Jauna Jaunas come too driving down from the mountainside this morning; they're all in Sunday clothing. Aile's jacket is snow-white, made of reindeer calfskin, and on the inside too it is soft and white as silk. Her Sámi boots are snow-white; her leggings are densely haired and shiny black; the red artistically woven bands are wound painstakingly beautifully around the leg of the Sámi boots. She has an old, fine silk shawl over her shoulders, and the little blue silk kerchief on her head is tied in a bowknot at the neck. Her hair peeks out golden and light and glorious.

Olle goes over and unties her reindeer. He ties it to a post and gets a *limpu* for it.

People have a certain weakness for such, – for such they're ready to yield in spite of everything.

Saivo Piera is also here. It is just old Saivo who is missing, – the miracle had in a way not wanted to allow himself to be driven out of his magpie nest on the plateau.

Jauna Jauna had with Anda Juoksa – he who brought the letter to Olle in the fall – sent a message to the sheriff that he, Jauna Jauna, had unfortunately happened to fall into error in an offense.

The Saivos had been reported by a traveler who had surprised them late in August, and old Saivo was besides reported for having threatened the traveler if the latter didn't want to keep his knowledge private.

But it wasn't just Saivos' and Jauna Jaunas' offenses that had moved the clergy and the sheriff's authorities to show up in such numbers here at Helligskogen. Also the events from the spring, from the Easter meeting, and not least the rumor about Bittoš Hansa's death needed to be examined painstakingly. The rumors here from Helligskogen had gradually taken quite fantastic dimensions – the supervisor and leader of prayers, the former dentist Ole Jansson had without further ado settled into an arrangement with a young girl for the summer, and also his earlier illness and marital relationship was by rumor made up according to all good, old rules. – The artistic philosopher and author of 'Cheerful tTenacity' wasn't forgotten either.

And yet Olle could with clear conscience say to himself that everything had happened against his good will and without any sinister calculation whatsoever on his part; he had just acted as a sleep-deprived convalescent and he couldn't help it so many crazy things had been caused.

But otherwise people seemed to be busy with everything other than bitter memories or to be troubled by repentance and contrition. The ministers and sheriff's authorities and this first Sunday in Advent had transformed all of Helligskogen into a cozy township for one day. No outsider can suspect to what high degree the minister and the sheriff's presence made life complete for these people. The children feel like this when father and big brother are at home on a Sunday. Everything is sort of so big and secure.

But when the chief is honored some of it rubs off on his subordinates. Olle sexton had his esteem repaired in this way when both the ministers and both the sheriffs had seized the occasion to have their teeth treated, – they were even going to lengthen their stay here by two or three days. And already yesterday on Saturday Olle had been in full swing filling the clergy's and authorities' cavities.

"Did you hurt your arm?" the minister asks.

"It is paralyzed to some extent unfortunately," Olle says …

But otherwise Olle had the feeling that mostly reminded him of a deft convict who is used for a little of everything by those who hold their protective iron fist over him.

Yes, for the case or the cases had still not been touched – one would presumably wait until Monday with that and devote Sunday exclusively to church business.

Olle tried to save his composure as best he could; but that the ministers and sheriffs already had agreed on a position toward him, he seemed to understand from many things.

Aile stood out there in the yard more beautiful and prouder in her bearing than ever. She was an eyesight in Helligskogen.

... Then it rings from the chapel's steeple for the third time; the two ministers in vestments and both the sheriffs and Olle go at the head of the festively dressed, reindeer jacket congregation the way there.

The chapel is packed full; one of the ministers officiates at the altar, the other will preach. And Olle is sexton.

The introductory prayer in the choir door, the hymn, the old, ever beautiful collection and epistle, the Lord's blessing the young, handsome minister chants with an unusually beautiful voice, – the listening faces and sincerely receptive hearts from the valley and the level mountain plateaus far inside in this great wilderness –, the confession and again a hymn, preaching from the pulpit, about Jesus, God's only begotten son, – communion and wedding – baptism and again a hymn ... Lord, have thanks for your word and for all your vehicles of divine grace, thanks for giving us this chapel here in Helligskogen!

Olle couldn't help it; he battled the need to burst into tears – Helligskogen had gradually become so fervently dear to him ... he had to clench his teeth.

And now the graveyard was also consecrated; now the dead from last spring could rest in Christian ground.

And in the afternoon there was vespers. The ministers had asked Olle to deliver a little sermon. Well, Olle tried; but he acquitted himself rather badly; he hadn't gotten the gift, he said; they had to excuse him.

* *
*

Monday morning Olle and the minister from the East Parish sit alone in the small room.

"... And frankly speaking do you think you will be able to adapt here in Helligskogen?" the minister asks. "It is probably not really the right sphere for you, Jansen ..."

* *
*

Olle takes the train down the large, wide valley bulging with forests ... *The way* they had gotten from his father, those over there in the east village. Now Olle too had left behind *a way*; but it was probably of another sort. Yes, for the *Asiatic way*, it's so easy for it to cause difficulties when it individually surprises people from the west.

The train stops, and Olle remains sitting and gaping at the depot which is in national style. Well I'll be! ... Weren't these lines revenants of the magpie cut? – These triangles and rectangles ... the patches on the magpie people's reindeer jacket collars. Two giants in wolfskin fur coats, but bareheaded and with the struggling pig bristles shining in the sun, staggered around in morning intoxication. – They had been to Kristiania and sold shoes, had broken a mirror at the Grand and asked what it cost. And now they were standing on the platform and telling the farmers about their pilgrimage to Jerusalem. The magpie people of the third generation.

The train whistles …

Wolves

Matti Aikio (1872-1929), a Sámi from Karasjok, Finnmark, Norway, was one of the world's first indigenous writers. His 1904 novel *King Ahab – or Falk and Jenny* was published in Copenhagen. His first Norwegian novel, *In Reindeer Hide,* came out in 1906 four years before Johan Turi's *An Account of the Sámi.* Turi wrote in Sámi (with some help from Emilie Demant), whereas Aikio, who did not begin studying Norwegian formally until he was eighteen, spent most of the rest of his relatively short life in Kristiania (Oslo) writing in Norwegian. He wrote articles for newspapers and Christmas magazines as well as eight books of which six were novels. He was writing during a period of harsh assimilation and social Darwinism. His books were popular among Norwegians who were interested in those exotic people up north, but his books were less successful among his own people, in part because he saw the best way forward for the Sámi was to learn the majority language which was tantamount to his supporting assimilation.

The illustrations between sections of this novel as well as on the cover come from famous works by Olaus Magnus (Olof Månsson) (1490-1557). Olaus was the last Catholic archbishop of Sweden. After the success of the Protestant Reformation, Olaus was exiled in 1530 and his property in Sweden confiscated. He spent most of the remainder of his life in Rome. He created *Carta marina*, a marine map and description of the northern lands from 1527 to 1539, a portion of which is on the cover of this book. He then published in 1555 a monumental work of nearly one thousand pages on the history and folklore of Scandinavia entitled *Historia de Gentibus Septentrionalibus* which was translated into many languages. The illustrations were done by an Italian artist whose experience of the lands to his north was easily exceeded by his imagination. Lapps, a somewhat derogatory exonym for the Sámi, dates back roughly to the year 1000 originally in the eastern part of Scandinavia.

John Weinstock, Ph.D. from the University of Wisconsin in Madison, taught Scandinavian languages, Sámi culture and Wagner's operas at the University of Texas at Austin for many years and is now Emeritus Professor. He has translated a number of works from Norwegian and Swedish and published numerous articles on the Sámi and their origins.

Gunnar Gjengset is a Norwegian scholar, an aphorist and a playwright. He received his fil. dr. from the University of Umeå in Sweden with a dissertation on Matti Aikio. Gjengset earlier published *Dobbelt hjemløs*, a biography of Aikio. He is also the biographer of Gustav Vigeland, the famous Norwegian sculptor: *Forsteinet liv. En biografisk fortelling om Gustav Vigeland* (2000).

www.ingramcontent.com/pod-product-compliance
Lightning Source LLC
Chambersburg PA
CBHW081324020726
47506CB00005B/1172